RAVE REVIEWS FOR
MARY ANN MITCHELL!

"Mary Ann Mitchell writes expressionistic hallucinations in which fascination, Eros and dread play out elaborate masques."
    —Michael Marano, author of *Dawn Song*

"Mary Ann Mitchell is definitely somebody to watch."
    —Ed Gorman, author of *The Dark Fantastic*

THE VAMPIRE DE SADE
"Mitchell's writing is as elegant as a poem in one sentence, then vicious as a viper in the next. ...An underground heir to Anne Rice's throne."
    —*The Horror Fiction Review*

"Mitchell is able to write without the stuffiness that puffs out the majority of modern vampire novels and she can turn on the gruesomeness as [well] as anyone."
    —*Masters of Terror*

"Mary Ann Mitchell will make her readers cringe while they read the horror within her pages!"
    —*Huntress Reviews*

TAINTED BLOOD
"A uniquely twisted take on the undead."
    —*Romantic Times*

THE PREY

An object rolled past Miriam as if it had been kicked but she heard nothing else. No steps, no talking, no... *Wait*, she thought. Barely audible, the sound grew closer. She wished that she hadn't worn heels. If she needed to run they would slow her down. Remembering the man between the two parked cars, she considered kicking her shoes off, dropping the bag, and making an all-out run. If anyone watched they would think her crazy. On the other hand, her life meant more to her than what people thought.

Miriam dropped the bag onto the sidewalk and kicked off her pumps. She took one broad step before being tackled to the ground. Her hands went immediately to her skirt, hoping to prevent rape. The person above her only chuckled.

He began tearing at her throat, his long nails slashing at her flesh. She attempted to scream but he twisted her face into the cement beneath them. He pawed with one hand at her throat like an animal until finally she felt blood rolling across the front of her neck. He settled his body heavily upon hers and nuzzled his face into her neck, lapping, sucking, licking. But no breath touched her flesh. The thing didn't breathe....

IN THE
NAME OF THE
VAMPIRE

MARY ANN MITCHELL

LEISURE BOOKS   NEW YORK CITY

A LEISURE BOOK®

November 2005

Published by

Dorchester Publishing Co., Inc.
200 Madison Avenue
New York, NY 10016

ISBN 0-8439-5544-9

Visit us on the web at www.dorchesterpub.com.

IN THE
NAME OF THE
VAMPIRE

ONE

Come with me down to the River Seine. The rain is over, and the wet streets will only be dotted with a few Parisians and one or two hearty tourists. At this very early-morning hour, none of the cafés or booksellers guarding the Seine will be open. Even the floating restaurants that serve tempura or tacos will be hushed.

The air is crisp with the bone-chilling dampness that settles softly on our clothes. Woolens revert to musty earth odors and sparkle with dew drops. Under the streetlamps your hair is aglow with a halo of the drizzle left from the storm.

No, don't touch a curl. The frizz makes you look like a small child again. The innocence will protect us as we pass through the alleyways and cross the broad avenues, passing century-old buildings that grow darker and nobler with age.

Careful on the cobblestone streets, because they can

be slippery after a storm, and in the dark it is easy to trip on a raised brick.

Look across the street. Two drunks are attempting to make their way home. Before daylight, they probably will stumble into a doorway and sink down onto the floor to fall asleep. They will not catch cold, since they'll keep each other warm. But pray that God keeps them safe and sound from the shadows that hunt in the night.

We are not far from the Seine now, for I can smell a hint of sewage on this muggy night. Yes, still the skies need to empty, but for this short respite let's view the swelling river. Sometimes the river floods the streets on the Left Bank, blocking traffic from Saint-Michel to the Eiffel Tower. But the river has served the people of Paris well. In the past, grain and wine moved in boats across the water. Now police patrol in speed-boats, tourists float by with their cameras, tilting the tour boats toward one site after another, and there are the lucky few who inhabit the houseboats, as Anaïs Nin did decades before we came here.

Ah! There is the Seine, its polluted water still a swimming hole for the hardy.

The water looks peaceful tonight; however, it is not always like this. Winters can cause the Seine to whip into a troubled brew, and in every season bodies have been found floating patiently down the river waiting to be retrieved and taken to the morgue. A century ago, near a Normandy village, Léopoldine, Victor Hugo's daughter, fell from a boat and sank to her death in the

Seine. Even cars have been lifted out of its sludge.

Let's not think such morbid thoughts; instead we should be savoring the quiet solitude so rare in a city hungry for pleasure. By day the benches are full of the aged with bags of bread to feed the pigeons. At night lovers caress and kiss, refusing to worry about who sees them.

The river is 482 miles of magic. The ancient Gauls built a temple at the source of the river to the goddess Sequana. Eventually, the goddess's name evolved into the Seine. The Parisii, a Celtic tribe, gave its name to the city.

I love coming down to the Seine at night, although I never come alone. There are stories that haunt many of the residents of Paris. Over there is the Ile de la Cité. You can see the spires of Notre Dame, which is on the other side of the island. We face the Conciergerie, which served as a prison from 1391 until 1914. During the French Revolution, there were four thousand prisoners housed there. Marie Antoinette awaited her execution in a tiny cell, and Charlotte Corday was imprisoned there after she stabbed the revolutionary leader Marat while he was in his bath. The menacing building still retains its eleventh-century torture chamber. Even by daylight the building appears to loom over the Seine with sinister pride.

Wait! I think there is someone sleeping on the stones over there. But this person is too limp, too spread out to be sleeping in this chill. As I move closer, I see that it is a female and no mist of steam rises from her gaping mouth. She looks ghastly white under the spray of the streetlamp bulb.

Let's hurry home. There is nothing more to see tonight, and I certainly wish to meet no one who could cause us harm or embroil us in the secrets that poor soul keeps.

Two

Justin saw two figures move briskly away from the Seine. One kept looking over a shoulder, the other hustled so quickly that the figure almost tripped and fell. Neither noticed his dark form coming toward them, and he swiftly stepped behind a pissoir to avoid being seen. He wondered what these two fools were doing at this early morning hour. Barely two A.M.; both should be in bed with doors and windows locked.

Once the two people had disappeared, Justin stepped out of the darkness. Dressed in black, with a touch of white around his collar, he looked religious, a priest perhaps, in soaking wet clothes. He kept his tall frame erect and brushed back his flaxen hair, darkened by the night's rain. His face looked chalky from the long nights he had spent wandering the edges of the Seine seeking one special vampire. One that had obviously gone mad with his hunger, killing instead of merely tasting from his victims. Five had already died, two females and three males. The newspapers listed the females as known prostitutes. The males had been foreign with no arrest records, but the police questioned what the males were doing in a disreputable area skimming the Seine.

Justin took a few steps and then smelled the beginnings of rotting flesh. Dead no more than three hours, the body lay directly in his path. Coming upon the body, he stopped and made the sign of the cross. Not as his mother had taught him to do, for she had not, but as he had watched at many of the burials he had attended. Inevitably, as he walked the cemeteries he would on occasion come upon a fresh grave, the grievers still lingering, unable to separate themselves from the empty shell inside the coffin.

Justin squatted next to the body and saw the blank stare of a young woman who couldn't be more than twenty-five under the heavy makeup. The eyes were wide, and her mouth gaped open in surprise, in a scream, or perhaps to beg for pity. The perpetrator had shown none. Instead he had broken her neck and slit her throat at the jugular. Not typical of a vampire, he knew, but perhaps he didn't want blame to fall on his own kind. Who else would practically drain the body of its blood?

Justin's hand covered the victim's eyes, and he gently closed the eyelids, black mascara marring the palm of his hand. She had fought her attacker, as evidenced by her nose, which had been pushed to one side of her face, and her clenched fingers had a number of broken

6

nails. Her clothes were inexpensive but not lewd. Her shoes were missing; the stockings on her feet were shredded.

He stood. He must go home now and apologize to Madeline. She complained of being tired of his nightly outings, of his spying on the diseased, dark culture that existed way into the Paris night. Sometimes he listened to whispers that gossiped in the darkened crevices of the embankment.

Being half-vampire and half-human, Justin ached for his true identity but feared what the answer might be. Years before, he had staked his mother while she lay resting in her coffin. He thought this would give her peace. Instead, another vampire's spirit invaded his mother's body, using it to reenter the world.

The drizzle started to turn into raindrops. He felt the rain slide down his face, dripping onto his clothes. If he had shed tears, he would never know.

But he had Madeline, the softness of her skin, the sweet lilt of her voice, and the honeysuckle smell that she dabbed on after a bath. He loved her but would never dare consummate his love, for she might end up like the dead woman at his feet.

THREE

Justin climbed the stairs to the garret he shared with Madeline. His running shoes, a soggy mess of canvas and leather, stained the carpet with mud.

He stopped to search his pocket for the key and to shake his head at the silly witch Madeline had hung on the door. At the very tip of the witch's nose Madeline had colored in a mole. She had glued on several alley cat's hairs to the mole. The witch's fingers had been placed so that they pointed to the door knocker. Her clothes, a howl of color, brightened the door. Madeline said Joan of Arc, the witch, would protect the garret. Justin had insisted that it was irreverent to name the witch after a saint.

"But Joan of Arc was burned at the stake as a witch," she said calmly.

"She is a saint, not a witch."

"How would you know the difference? And who are

you to judge a witch? You speak as though all witches are evil. I think not. In the village where I grew up, there was an old woman who practiced witchcraft and made some dreadful-tasting potions that healed the sick."

"The sick were lucky they didn't die."

"Anything tasting that bad had to be good for you."

"I take it you were one of her patients."

"My brother, me, and even our father. Mother always avoided the foul-smelling tonics."

"Wise woman," Justin said.

Madeline threw her towel at him, revealing the curves of her freshly bathed body. The vision won her the argument, since his mind went totally blank with lust.

Justin paused a second to erase the image. They had cuddled, caressed, and kissed, but never went beyond that. He feared his loss of control. Feared the possibility that he, too, could harbor the hunger for blood.

He unlocked the door and pushed it inward. The creak and whine made him hold his breath and raise his shoulders as if those instinctive movements could somehow bring silence. The lights were out, and the air held a slight odor of the fish they had had for dinner. Before he had left, he had made her promise to shut and lock all the windows. Her grimace had prepared him for lingering odor. He closed the door and locked both locks, which she had forgotten to do. *She'll never learn,* he thought. Either she trusted too easily, or she reacted with bravado to his warnings. She was deter-mined to show her independence.

A canvas and iron screen hid the bed from his view. Diagonally across the room, dishes had been piled on the marble counter for drying. The frying pan lay soak-ing in the sink.

He slipped quickly into the bathroom to get ready for bed. He waited until he had closed the door before switching on the light. The laundry had disappeared, which was unusual since Madeline would leave it up until morning to ensure that mildew would not grow on the fabrics. The toothbrushes had been swept into the sink by a careless, hurried movement. He returned them to their proper places and finished his bedtime chores.

After turning the light off, he opened the door and slowly moved across the oak floor toward the bed. The moonless night prevented his spying Madeline before he got into bed. He reached gently to her side, hoping not to awake her. His hand fell on wrinkled sheets. He grabbed her pillow and easily spilled it onto the floor.

Panicked, Justin tried to find the bedside lamp, but instead he heard it crash to the floor.

"Madeline," he yelled, rising from the bed to find the wall light switch.

The bright ceiling light came on like a flashbulb and held the room in a momentary stillness until Justin's eyes were able to adjust.

"Madeline," he yelled once more, looking around the garret. "Don't play games." As if searching for a small child, Justin looked under the bed and in their mid-sized armoire. Clothes were gone. Not all of them, but enough to make him understand that she had left.

"Where would she go?" he said out loud.

She had made several friends in the building, all female, all older than she.

He went to the window and looked down on a deserted street. He stood there for five or ten minutes, but not even a car rumbled by.

Laying the palms of his hands flatly against the windowpane, Justin tried to calm himself. Why would she have left him? Other than their typical argument about his wandering the paths along the Seine, they never fought. They didn't have much money except for the few hundred euros Madeline kept hidden in one of her shoes. Justin crossed back to the armoire and searched. The shoes were gone, but he caught sight of a wad of bills sticking out of one of his old jackets. He counted the money, exactly half of what they had saved. He wished she had taken it all. He dropped the money on the floor. When had she left? Even though she had asked him not to leave, could she really have been waiting for him to go?

Madeline would never return to her parents' small town, for surely they knew about her affair with Sade and the evil he had brought to the town's cathedral. Besides, she loved Paris. She had even started sculpting classes with one of the local artists. The artist. Justin felt a twinge of jealousy. The middle-aged artist fawned over her work, encouraging her to spend more time at his studio. From the brief glimpse Justin had of her work, it seemed she needed to learn far more than the artist's praise would have led one to believe.

Jacques, the man with the graying head of curls and the full, virile beard, would often telephone in the evenings to follow up on her progress. Always giddy after the call, Madeline would immediately turn to her sketching, refusing to take walks or even sit quietly with Justin.

But how could Justin blame her? Feeling tired, he wandered over to the bed and sat. He looked at the sheets, which were still wrinkled from the night before, when she had held him close. Sometimes she grasped him so hard that he felt a slight ache around his ribs in the morning.

Justin lay back and rested his head on the down pillow. He pulled her pillow atop himself and breathed in her honeysuckle odor. Hugging the pillow to his chest, he closed his eyes. The pillow did not weigh nearly enough to approximate her body, but still it prevented the chill of the room from contacting his body. The radiator clanged, and Justin rolled over on top of the pillow, burying his face to cut off the eruption of tears.

FOUR

In the morning, Justin's stiff body didn't want to get out of bed. His right arm had fallen asleep under the pressure of his body. His left hand tried to rub the sleep from his eyes, to no avail. Instead, his hand felt the indentation in his skin where the folds of the pillow had impressed themselves.

Why couldn't she have faced him? At least she could have said good-bye before packing her clothes. She had been the one who had demanded they go to Paris; otherwise, he would have returned to New Orleans, where he had . . .

He thought for several minutes and couldn't remember anything he had left. Not even his mother was interred there now.

Madeline had fallen in love with the garret. The small size didn't matter as long as she had the sun shining through the window in the early afternoon, making it easier for her to sketch.

Justin rolled onto his back and cursed the sun, the garret, even the screen that took up too much room.

The sourness in his mouth made him thirsty, but his legs wouldn't cooperate. They lay weighted and semi-numb against the sheet. He could no longer smell the fish but knew the odor still lingered in the air, waiting to turn his stomach. He pushed his body out of bed, unlocked the windows, and threw them fully open. Children with backpacks paraded down the street. The school a block away, was in session; therefore, he knew it couldn't be Sunday.

A knock on the front door made his body jolt. Throwing a robe over his naked body, he crossed the room and opened the door.

"Hi," said the older woman from down the hall. "Madeline said she would mind my grandson this morning."

He looked down by her side and saw big brown eyes that reminded him of a cocker spaniel. The boy seemed to be barely two years old and had just recently learned to walk, judging by the sway of his plump body.

"She isn't here."

"*Mais non,* she promised. I offered to pay even, but she refused the money, saying she would enjoy having company."

Huge kettle drums started to pound inside his head. He flung the door fully open.

"Madame, do you see Madeline?"

14

The woman cautiously peered into the apartment. "Is she in bed still?"

Justin crossed the room and knocked the screen to the floor. When he turned back to the door, there was no one at the threshold.

FIVE

Jacques rested his head on the derriere of his newest student. The minx played at being asleep, but he knew she just wanted to be allowed to stay longer. Alas, that couldn't be, since he had a prospective buyer coming within the hour.

"I warned you last night, my angel, that you couldn't stay for breakfast."

He heard her snore loudly and laughed.

"Later in the week, we shall have another lesson. Perhaps you could bring a few croissants, and I will supply the coffee."

She rubbed her face into the pillow and continued to ignore him.

He raised himself up and walloped her behind hard.

Her scream proved that she could no longer ignore his pleas.

"Up, up. Today I expect to make enough to pay my rent for a change. Maybe have a little left over to buy a gift for my favorite pupil. Hmmmm. Certainly, Margarete deserves a reward for her style, or even Lisa for the suppleness of her fingers."

Finally, his bedmate lifted up her head and issued a loud raspberry.

"Why must you tease me with those awful girls? None have my talents," she said, turning the upper part of her body to display her plump, upright breasts.

"Ah, but they sketch far more than you do. You waste time dreaming about the work you want to do instead of putting effort into designing a masterpiece."

"Jacques," she said, moving herself into a seated position. "The masterpiece is in my head. I can see it clearly. The shading. The texture. The curves."

"The bullshit you spout." He leaned over the side of the bed and came back with a bundle of clothes. "Here. Perhaps you could shower when you get home. My shower isn't working so well anyway. It's impossible to regulate the hot water."

She took the clothes from him and sat in a sulk.

"No! My work comes first, young lady, as it should for you also." He bounced out of bed and headed for the bathroom. "The door will lock automatically."

"Hmpf," he heard as he closed the door.

He hadn't lied about the shower water. Every few minutes the temperature changed, depending on whether someone else in the building was washing or using the toilet. He finally simply turned the water to cold and rushed through the shower.

By the time he returned to the bedroom, she had

left. He sighed with relief and began singing a popular tune. He drew on his jeans and pulled a T-shirt over his head. The contours of his muscles filled out the shirt. He shunned his sandals in favor of bare feet and wandered down the long hall, intending to make fresh coffee, but the doorbell rang.

Too early, he thought, checking the grandfather clock next to the front door. However, it would not be the first time that an anxious client arrived before the appointed hour. The more anxious the client, the higher the price he could charge.

He opened the door and found a tall youth hovering over him. The young man looked a bit familiar but certainly couldn't be the client. His creased clothes could be a hint that he slept in the streets.

"If you're selling anything . . ."

"I'm looking for someone. A woman with whom I . . ." The young man hesitated.

"Have a relationship?" the artist assisted.

"Live." The young man's voice sounded harsh.

"Why would she be here, then?" Jacques thought of the newest student and moaned softly to himself. He hated complications.

"She didn't sleep at home last night."

"Maybe if you go back home now, she will have returned with a good excuse for her—"

A pot fell in the kitchen, and he heard his student curse in a loud voice.

"Then again, there is never an excuse that will placate any man." Jacques beckoned the visitor in and led the way to the kitchen.

The student knelt on the marble floor of the kitchen, attempting to pick up scrambled eggs.

"I couldn't know that she had someone waiting," Jacques explained, walking around the student to put coffee on the stove.

"Where is she, then?"

Jacques looked over his shoulder at the visitor and pointed toward the girl. Both the visitor and the girl looked at him, waiting for an explanation.

"Isn't she the girl you're looking for?"

The student and the visitor looked at each other, trying to place faces.

Finally, the visitor spoke the key word. "Madeline."

"Madeline?"

"Another one," said the student.

"Clean that up and make some eggs for both of us, angel, while I speak with the young man."

"Who's Madeline?" the student cried out.

Jacques didn't bother to answer. He ushered the man out of the kitchen and into the parlor.

With the drapes drawn and the sun filling the living room, he was able to get a better look at the visitor.

The features were almost perfect, the eyes a shade of green the artist had never seen before. Jacques wished that such color existed within the spectrum of his paints. The visitor was a good six foot one or two, his build slender but not delicate. He seemed strong, and his long fingers kept opening and closing. The complexion, though, could belong to a dead man.

"Justin," Jacques blurted out. "Madeline's lover. Yes, I met you once, I believe, at her first class."

SIX

Justin nodded, looking down at the five-foot-five artist. Jacques had a bulky build but had no fat. Instead, he seemed to be made up of muscle and gristle. He wore his clothes tight to emphasize his strength. His face wore a mask of laugh lines and worry lines.

"You mean Madeline has left you?" A certain glee clung to his words.

"You tell me."

The artist shrugged and settled himself on the charcoal velvet sofa, his feet sinking comfortably into the cushions.

"Why would I know? Do you think she is here? Explore the apartment; you will find only a spoiled child whose parents pay me well to keep her entertained and ignorant of her lack of talent."

"There's no place else she would go. She respects your advice."

"And that means she would come here. No, not

here. She loves you, or at least that is what I had thought."

The student entered the room with a tray filled with eggs, fruit, and stale biscuits.

"I made enough for everyone," she said, setting the tray on the dining table. "Your visitor doesn't look like he's had a decent meal today."

"I doubt he has the appetite to eat, my angel. No problem, though, I'm famished and will eat his share."

The doorbell rang.

"Another client?" the student asked.

"Justin is not a client. He is a man on a quest to find his lover."

"Madeline," the student murmured.

"Yes. Do you know her?" Justin asked.

"Don't care to," she said, crunching into a biscuit.

Jacques had left the room, and when he returned he had a woman dressed in black in tow. A dark veil covered her face, and she halted warily in the doorway.

"My angel has prepared breakfast for three, madame. Perhaps you would like to join us?"

The veiled woman nodded toward Justin.

"He isn't hungry. Well, not for food."

"For love," clarified the student.

The veiled woman turned to leave.

"Wait," Justin called out. "I'll be leaving so that you may carry out your business." Turning toward Jacques, he asked, "When did you last see Madeline?"

"Two days ago when she had her last class. I didn't expect to see her until this Friday. Does this mean I have an empty slot to fill? I don't mean to be crude, but I can't afford to waste my time."

"I could use an extra class," the student volunteered.

"If she comes here, will you call me?" Justin asked.

"I'll mention that you were here, but I hardly want to get involved with your lover's quarrel."

"We didn't fight. We disagreed about my going out in the evening."

"Every woman wants her man feeding the fireplace and massaging her ego." Jacques smiled.

As Justin turned to leave, the veiled woman moved into the bathroom and closed the door.

SEVEN

Justin waited across the street from the artist's town house. The tall windows served as mirrors, reflecting the activity taking place on the street. He watched the pigeons roost in the decorative crevices under the eaves of the roof. The double wood doors at the entrance of the house remained shut for at least an hour before the student exited, a canvas bag thrown over one shoulder and a thick cashmere sweater over the other. Her slender legs rode high on six-inch heels, causing her to wobble slightly as she walked up the street.

But he waited for the woman in the veil. He had recognized something familiar about her. Could she be Madeline? Should he go back and face her and Jacques? His stomach churned with doubts and fear. Finally, the door opened and the veiled woman walked out onto the street. As she walked, he realized she didn't have Madeline's body build. And the bit of hair sticking out of her hat looked too dark.

He almost began to follow, and then he saw her get into a waiting cab.

Why torture himself? he wondered. If she didn't want to be with him anymore, there seemed to be no purpose in playing private detective. He spent the next several hours wandering the streets, attempting to walk off his pain. He refused to return to the garret and remained on the street until dark, when he headed down to the Seine.

The clear skies and near-balmy temperatures brought out hungry denizens of the night who felt cheated by the previous night of famine. They gloried in the renewal of available blood, smiling and joking with their prey. Too excited to control himself, one vampire couldn't keep from salivating as the parade of humans passed by. Most of the vampires stayed close to the bridges, where a moment of quiet could allow a shove into a dark nook.

"He's back, you know. Been back for weeks. Has already settled into his visiting of private clubs and parties."

"I avoid him whenever I can," returned a softer voice.

"Really! I've always found Sade entertaining," the harsher, colder voice replied.

Justin came close to walking away when he caught the next sentence.

"He has a young woman with him now. Very young. She has marvelous hair and the perfect body. However, she holds herself aloof and rarely accompanies Sade. I've only seen her a couple of times. I couldn't swear that they live together. She may only see him on occasion."

"Perhaps she is not one of us."

"I haven't gotten close enough to tell. Pardon me."

Justin jostled the vampire, almost knocking him off his feet. The vampire attempted to step out of the way, but Justin reached out and grabbed him by his corduroy jacket.

"I need to know about this woman who is with Sade," Justin said.

The other vampire backed into a cluster of bushes and disappeared.

Justin grasped the jacket tighter, and the vampire squinted his eyes, staring into Justin's green ones.

"You're a half-breed, aren't you. Do you want to be turned completely?"

"No. The woman who is with Sade—I need to know whether she is there willingly."

The vampire pulled away from Justin.

"How would I know? You must have heard while eavesdropping that I didn't get a chance to speak with the woman. Didn't even get within ten feet of her."

"Where did you see her?"

"Champs-Elysées. They were going into the Grand Palais to visit the new exhibition. A wonderful display. . . ."

26

"When did you see them?"

"You'll never get her back. If she hasn't been turned already, she will be. They looked very comfortable together. I had never seen them together before, but they seemed to be old friends. They laughed loudly and held each other's hand."

"When?"

"Two evenings ago. Just before that killer storm. Personally, I don't care for half-breed blood, but I do have a friend with odd taste buds. You'd probably have a better chance at getting her back if you were turned."

"My goal is to bring her back before she is turned, monsieur."

The vampire shook his head.

"Sade will kill you if you take anyone or anything that belongs to him. You'll never survive."

"I believe the woman you saw is a person that I've taken away from him, and I stand before you."

"Maybe they were amused by you. Making you think you had won. If this is the woman you are looking for, she is not wasting her time on thoughts of you."

Justin shivered. "No, she wanted to escape from her old life. She wouldn't go back to him."

"Your brains are bubbling over with love, making it impossible for you to see reality. Why, monsieur, would she want to come back to a half-breed? Especially a poverty stricken one. Sade's clothes are finer than the rags you wear. He is old and wise, with money collected over several centuries. Unfortunate that he hadn't been turned at your age, but he doesn't grow any older. As we talk, your body decays. Organs are deteriorating. Flesh is beginning to sag and crinkle into lines. Ah, monsieur, she is too full of herself. Find someone better."

"Where can I find Sade?"

"Anywhere that is polluted with the ravings of lost souls. Pick a club that offers the sweat and blood of the masochistic. Indulge in a brothel with illicit tastes. I doubt you'll gain admittance to the more vicious parties. They are very private."

"There is no one place?"

The vampire smirked. "None of us leave our prints or post our itinerary on bathroom walls. Any who do are destroyed."

EIGHT

"Are we supposed to starve to death while your mother parties at your aunt's?"

"The celebration should be over by now, Dad."

"Then where is she? What is it, two blocks to your aunt's house?"

"Three and a half," said the ten-year-old girl, her back against the oak floor and her feet resting on the cushions of the sofa.

"We could get some fast food," suggested the girl's fifteen-year-old brother.

"My stomach jumps for joy at that idea. Oh, wait, I'm wrong. It merely threatens to run away from home," said the father.

The girl giggled, but her brother rose to leave the room.

"Since you are up, Matthew, would you mind—"

"I'm not cooking anything, Dad."

"I wouldn't eat whatever you'd cook. Not while

you're such a gourmet of fast food. No, I'd like you to rescue your mother."

The boy shrugged. "Maybe she doesn't want to come home."

"Go," the father demanded, allowing the newspaper to fall to the floor.

Before his father could rise and take a swipe at him, Matthew threw on a light jacket and left the apartment. He dug into his pockets and found an old lollipop his sister had asked him to hold. Unraveling the notepaper around the pop, Matthew skipped down the front stairs. He tossed the paper onto the sidewalk, stuck the pop into his mouth, and considered running away from home for the three hundred and ninetieth time. They'd miss him. They'd be sorry. Especially Mom, knowing she caused his flight. Hell, maybe he'd wait until his father paid for college.

As he stepped off the curb, he saw a wiry young man start to dart out from an alleyway up ahead, but he retreated as soon as he saw Matthew. Matthew thought about turning back or taking another way to his aunt's house. A car honked as he barely stopped in the middle of the street.

"You too," he yelled back at the driver, even though he hadn't heard what had been said. Everybody told him what to do. Some skinny guy in an alleyway had him thinking about going several blocks out of his way. Why? The guy didn't own the street. Besides, when he got near the alleyway he could walk out where the cars were. Not that he'd scamper away like a coward. But the distance would enable him to see trouble coming and prepare.

Matthew continued down the street, debating in his head whether he should briefly leave the sidewalk before he reached the alley. Eventually, he found himself within a couple of feet of the alley and he heard nothing. Veering slightly toward a parked car, he continued on until he saw a paisley kerchief lying in the street. It looked a hell of a lot like the one he and his sister had given to their mother. Had she been wearing it when she left the house? He couldn't recall. Maybe she had dropped it and was already home. That couldn't be, since he hadn't passed her.

The kerchief lay inches away from the opening to the alley. He passed it by, but doubled back, thinking that anyone in the alley wouldn't expect him to return so soon. This time he stayed close to the building, within reaching distance of the kerchief. As he bent to pick up the paisley silk, he noticed an open hand at the mouth of the alley. The soft pink color of the nails matched his mother's.

Sweating fiercely and breathing hard, he froze.

"Mom," he called in a hushed voice. His eyes were already watering. "Are you all right, Mom?"

A breeze came and wrapped the scarf around Matthew's ankles, almost tripping him as he took a step closer to the hand.

"Mom." He peered into the alley and saw a woman's figure lying on the ground. He recognized the clothes, but the face lay in the shadow of the stone wall.

"Mom." He heard his own voice quiver, and he began to kneel.

A dark shape flew out of an indentation in the opposite wall. Matthew tried to rise, but the mass pounced heavily on top of him, knocking his breath out of him and causing him to fall on the cooling body of his mother, recognizable now as his outstretched hand turned her face toward him.

"He's a child. Leave him alone," came a woman's soft voice.

NINE

Justin watched the young girls gyrate to the music and the males plot their moves. The Goth culture had died down a bit in the clubs. He wondered how this would affect the vampires who preyed on Goth youths. The vampires were still present, but many had changed their attire, attempting to fit in with the prey. Several seemed more comfortable in their new clothes, happy to be rid of the heavy cloaks, velvets, and dark colors they had worn for centuries.

The young woman next to him had been plying two men with drinks all night, but neither male had any interest in leaving with her. Her bulk and poor French ensured another night of blood hunger. Justin thought that she had made a poor choice, since the males were probably going home together.

"I'm so bored with this club scene. Aren't you?"

A blond woman held Justin's arm. Her voice sounded rough, as if she were a smoker.

"Then why do you come here?" he asked.

"To meet bored men like you." She raised her eyebrows.

"True, I am bored of these haunts."

She sniffed his body.

"A half-breed. But you are good-looking. Are you shy?"

"I've spent most of my life alone."

"Because you are ashamed of what you are?"

"I don't know what I am."

"Neither mortal nor undead." She squeezed his arm. "Why not leave with me?"

"And where would you take me? Down by the Seine where you can satiate yourself on my blood?"

"There have been murders tonight," she said.

"And what do you know of them?"

"Nothing. There are murders every night. Sometimes lovers make final a separation. Sometimes strangers mistake a slight for an evil deed. Children kill to prove themselves. The elderly want to relieve pain. Come home with me tonight, for I want to die."

"You are beyond death. Your body can be destroyed, but you'll still exist. Oblivion is impossible." Justin felt the weight of his sadness close the lids of his eyes.

"You're not seeking gaiety tonight, monsieur. Why come out? To make the rest of us mourn with you?"

"To remind you of your sins," he said, opening his eyes to find a spotlight directed at him.

The woman leaned closer to him and whispered.

34

"We know who you are. We have watched you kill our kind."

The music stopped and the patrons circled him. The confused mortals felt abandoned, ignored suddenly by suitors.

"You lied. You don't want to die. You want to kill me," he said.

"Leave us alone, half-breed. Stop walking the cemeteries and the alleys. Quit hugging the Seine. Go far away and you will live your petty life. Otherwise, our tolerance will snap, and you will die not as one of us but as the weak, impotent man you are."

"Why hasn't one of you killed me already?"

"There is a rumor that you walk in Sade's shadow. If he has allowed you to live, there must be a reason. You sleep with a woman he once kept."

"Not anymore. He has taken her back."

The woman turned his face to her and searched his features for truth. Her long nails scraped the side of his face.

"And will you seek her?" she asked.

"That is what I'm doing here. I've been told that Sade is back in Paris and visiting all the very best perverted places in this city."

"You'll not find him here. This place is too tame for him. There's a brothel. Slaves are kept there. Most are foreign. None will survive their days. Death comes easily to the men and women who work in this brothel. Most wear scars on their flesh and wounds on their souls that will never heal. Branding is a minor punishment there. Gossip says that some mortals have been flayed alive to entertain the most jaded vampires. Dollops of flesh dripping with blood are munched as snacks."

"Where is this place?"

She leaned closer. Her lips touched the curves of his ear.

"I can take you there. Leave with me and the others will not harm you."

Justin glanced at the crowd. All the eyes were darkened with hate. One old man sniffed his cognac and nodded at Justin. The old face didn't hold familiar features, but the stoop of his shoulders reflected the gravity of his age.

"Marissa, let the young man be," said the old man.

Justin heard the woman groan and felt her hands slowly release him.

"Quick, tell me the name of the brothel and its address," Justin demanded, holding both her hands inside his strong fists.

The woman spat in his face. She had bitten the inside of her mouth, causing saliva and blood to be mixed.

The old man had been moving closer to them until finally he laid his cold hands on Justin's wrists.

"She can't tell you what she doesn't know, monsieur."

"But she said . . ."

"Look at her face, monsieur. Doesn't she look capable of telling lies?"

She smiled, and her front teeth were tinged with blood.

"I need to find Sade."

"He wants to rescue his girlfriend from our community." The woman dug her nails into the palms of Justin's hands.

"You may start a riot, monsieur," said the old man.

Justin looked down and saw blood bubble up between his fingers. Immediately, he set the woman free. She snapped at him as a teased dog might do.

In a side booth, hidden by a burgundy, velvet curtain, sat a woman peering out of a small niche. She didn't like the way Justin's voice carried or the fuss he had made. *Let time sleep in its grave, idiot. Don't pick at ancient wounds that have stopped festering. Go back to New Orleans.*

She had her back to a lover, one of many that she had recently taken. His blistered hands caressed her smooth back, making her skin prickle at his touch. His tongue lapped at the sensitive skin behind her right ear. Still she ignored him, watching the delicate balance taking place on the main floor.

"I am Gerard," the old man said, offering his hand. "And you are the terror in our nightmares."

"Your hands are too cold for me to touch, monsieur."

Gerard frowned and acted perturbed, but Justin knew it was an act. The sly old man hadn't interfered solely to save Justin's life. He wanted something.

"Justin, there are no free tables here. Why don't we find a quieter bar? One without the loud music. I'm way too old for this place."

"Then why do you come here, Gerard?" Marissa asked.

"To irritate the hell out of you, Marissa. I succeed every time, don't I?"

She waved a hand at Gerard and walked away. Once she had left, the crowd dispersed.

"Justin, I believe we can help each other, but talking here is impossible. These children may have dispersed, but they still cannot take their eyes off of you. We need to leave and find a place that knows neither of us. And just such a place has opened on the Rue de Rivoli." Gerard grabbed Justin's elbow and ushered the half-breed to the exit.

No matter how much he resisted, Justin couldn't pull away from Gerard's grip, and he found himself lurching out the door.

"A cab, or shall we walk?" Gerard asked. "We can talk while walking. I wouldn't dare air our secrets within the confines of a taxi. By this time of the evening, the drivers are bored and can't help but to catch every word we say, even if we whisper. Rue de Rivoli is but a mile from here, and that is nothing for us. Agreed?"

"What do you want from me, monsieur?"

"Your help; and you need my help to find Sade."

"He never keeps a low profile."

"But it still could take you days, perhaps weeks, to

find him. Does she have that long? If he truly grows fond of her, then . . ." Gerard snapped his fingers.

"Where will I find Sade?"

"No, no, Justin. I don't do charity. I expect payment."

"How much?"

"Not money. Your time and expertise."

"Ah, Gerard, you are still with the brave vampire slayer. Won't you share his exotic blood with us," said Marissa.

Several young vampires laughed.

Justin turned and saw Marissa and several of her . . . friends? No, he thought, they were more likely accomplices.

"You see, Justin, it is impossible to get any privacy here. Marissa is the neighborhood thugess. She roams these streets seeking trouble or creating it. She doesn't stray very far, though. Isn't that right, Marissa?"

She stuck out her tongue at Gerard.

"Marissa is an infant among our breed, although she has managed to collect quite a fan club through her own carelessness."

"I made these blood children, Gerard. You are jealous because you don't dare make any of your own."

"I am much too cautious, Marissa, to pick up random school kids on the street. They have parents who will search for them, and you leave our society vulnerable to the human world."

Marissa mocked Gerard with a sulky pout.

"I hate being chastised by anyone, but especially by you, Gerard."

"Go home, Marissa. You don't want to play this scene out." The elderly man stood relaxed, his hands inside the pockets of his corduroy jacket that matched his trousers.

Marissa's eyes shifted toward Justin. He watched her chest puff up and her eyes flash with hate and desire before she leaped at him.

In the split second that he steeled himself, her body fell to the cement sidewalk. The gaping hole in her chest shed hardly any blood. He looked at Gerard and watched as the elderly man wrapped her heart inside a handkerchief.

Her vampire children stood stunned and still.

"Listen to me," Gerard shouted at the vampires. "Take her body and bury it deep in the ground. Take the heart and burn it separately. And make sure you separate her head from her body."

No one moved.

"Now. Do it now unless you wish to follow your mistress into hell."

One of the vampires stepped forward. The short, petite female fell to her knees before Gerard.

"Please, she hadn't taught us everything we need to know, lord. We need a teacher."

"You've learned enough to survive on the outskirts of our community, and that is all you deserve." He pressed the bulky handkerchief into her hands. He used the scarf around Marissa's neck to clean off his hands.

"Justin, let's depart from here before we attract a mob," he murmured.

They had started down the block when Justin said, "You didn't have to kill her."

"And what would you have done if she had buried her teeth in your neck?"

"I would have killed her first."

"So what's the difference?"

"She didn't try to destroy you."

"Lord, no, not a moralist. If you wish to outwit Sade, you'll have to banish your morals for a while."

"I've defeated him before."

"I have the feeling he'd be destroyed if you had." Gerard smirked and looped his arm with Justin's as they traveled on to the Rue de Rivoli.

TEN

Gerard and Justin sipped their drinks and sized each other up. The talk up to this point had been sparse. Gerard had been content to take in the night air and let Justin mull over his options, which were not many.

"For how long has this woman been with you?"

"How long doesn't matter. She trusted me to keep her safe."

"Ah, soul mates. And what was she to Sade?"

Justin's gut soured, and he wondered why he sat in a dimly lit bar talking to this vampire who probably couldn't help him find Madeline. The ancient vampire sat peering at Justin, waiting for a reply, or perhaps simply trying to make a point.

"I don't have time to waste, monsieur. I must find Madeline before . . ."

Gerard allowed a moment of complete silence before he spoke.

"As I remember, Sade tired of his play toys quickly. What is so special about Madeline that he would return for her?"

Justin attempted to stand, but Gerard pulled him back down.

"A stupid question. You wouldn't let her go. Why should Sade?"

"I just want to know that she left willingly and is not with Sade. I'll not force her to come back to me."

Gerard nodded.

"You and she have never made love?"

"I told you, she trusts me to protect her."

"Even from you. Have you thought about crossing over completely?"

"I would never do that."

"But you're afraid that the vampire half could overcome the human part of you."

"It has happened."

"Did you like the taste of blood?"

Justin's hand gripped his glass tightly, and he felt it shatter into pieces, piercing his own flesh. Blood seeped from between his fingers. Gerard's lips shivered almost imperceptibly.

A waitress came to their table carrying a clean dish towel.

"Monsieur, come to the bathroom and let me wash your wound." She grabbed his hand, and he furiously pulled away from her.

"She is merely trying to help, Justin. Let her wash

your hand. I'm too disturbed by the sight of blood to do what is needed."

Justin realized he had become just as much the center of attention as he had been at the club. He thanked the waitress and followed her.

ELEVEN

Jacques rolled over in bed and felt the warmth of smooth flesh. Who shared his bed this night? he wondered. He must have had plenty of wine with dinner, because he couldn't remember.

Madeline's image arose from the depths of his mind. He saw her filled with enthusiasm, intent on his words and movements, and careful not to spoil her work. The deep lines that formed between her eyebrows while sculpting, the way her lips pursed when she made a sharp curve in the clay, or the way her chest ceased to rise and fall when she awaited his criticism. Oh, and the luscious breasts that touched his forearms when he reached around her to guide her fingers.

His foreskin tightened around his swollen penis. He thought about reaching down to satisfy himself when he remembered the warm body next to him. Couldn't be Madeline, he thought, she had seemed inured to all his casual flirtations.

The dark room prevented him from seeing whether the woman next to him had blond hair, brown, or Madeline's lovely red tresses. His hands searched the woman's body. The soft skin covered a voluptuous figure. Too voluptuous to be Madeline, but still warm and female and responsive.

Their bout of lovemaking was short, since he had been near orgasm when he entered her. She moaned briefly in disappointment, but soon he heard coarse snores and reached over to heave her onto her side. Immediately, she folded into a fetal position, and even though he couldn't quite make out her features in the dark, he would have sworn she sucked on one of her thumbs.

Unable to sleep, Jacques got out of bed and walked naked into his studio. The statue that had been bought that day stood in the center of the room, a white canvas cloth covering it.

He thought of the high price his client had paid, but still wondered whether he really wanted to give it up. He had secretly worked on the statue. No one besides his client and he himself had seen it. He had worked from memory and fantasy. The face obviously belonged to Madeline, but the body he had to imagine, since he had not dared to ask Madeline to pose. He had enjoyed molding her breasts and hips with his hands. The breasts fit perfectly into his large palms, and the hips were meant to breed many children. Not his, of course.

He wondered whether Madeline would show for her

next lesson free from the burden of love. If so, he might be able to compare his imagination with the reality of her.

Jacques removed the cloth from the statue and stood back to admire his work for the thousandth time. He decided he had sold the statue too cheaply, considering the long, tempting hours he had worked on this slab of clay. But he couldn't refuse to sell his Madeline now. Perhaps someday the warm-fleshed Madeline would take the statue's place.

He sat on the floor and leaned against the peeling wall to admire his dream of Madeline. Within a few minutes his head began to nod, but he quickly awoke to the sound of someone calling his name. Jacques immediately got to his feet, picked up the canvas cloth, and covered his masterpiece.

He threw a kiss to his Madeline from the doorway before rejoining his current guest in the bedroom.

TWELVE

Justin kept his head down as he returned to Gerard's table. The waitress had been able to staunch the blood with a few towels. His flesh always healed quickly. His vampire mother's legacy, no doubt.

"I ordered another round while you were gone. I presume the cuts are nothing serious. Certainly for a vampire they would be terribly minor, and you are part—"

"Don't remind me, Gerard." Justin sat down on the bronze-colored chair. "I came here to find out where Sade is. You implied that you knew, but now I believe you're a liar."

Gerard shook his head. "I've been cruel to you, Justin. There's a part of me that resents the way you deny your own kind."

"I am not a vampire. I don't survive on the blood of humans."

"I don't have to kill to survive. I don't eat mortal flesh. Look at the table next to us. For heaven's sake, I'm not going to attack you if you look away from me. Look at that burger the man at the next table is eating. See how much he's enjoying it. An animal had to die so that he could have those animal juices sliding down his chin."

"The man is a slob." Justin looked back at Gerard. "That's all I see. Besides, you said that you don't have to kill, but I bet that you have."

"There is a certain thrill in draining life from a mortal. But it's foolish and irresponsible to kill. That is why Marissa had to be destroyed. Her children were learning bad habits."

"Have you killed mortals?"

"Of course I have, Justin. Haven't you?"

"Twice in the midst of passion."

"While you were making love?"

Justin nodded.

"Hence the reason you won't make love to Madeline. It can be controlled. You just have to think less about your own pleasure and more about the woman's. If you truly love Madeline selflessly, no harm with come to her."

"I'll not take that risk."

"All the limitations you put on yourself make you look like a very sour young man. Indeed you are handsome, but you look like you've never known happiness. And I fear that you never will."

"Pity yourself, Gerard. You must live centuries with the killing and maiming you perform. And at the end of your existence, there'll be nothing and no one waiting for you."

"Does God wait for you, Justin? Do you proudly walk into church on Sundays, kneel in a pew, wrap rosary beads around your fingers, and share a personal talk with God?"

"I'm damned and I know it."

"Then why not enjoy what you have here on this earth? Are you hoping God will change his mind about you? Make an exception for the half-and-halves? But if he does that for you, what about me? You think you could intercede? As a friend—"

Justin raised his right hand to halt Gerard.

"You will never be my friend. Vampires are my enemies. You saw the way they treated me at the club tonight."

"Maybe if you stopped destroying them they'd have a change of heart."

"Is that why I'm here? You want to talk me out of staking vampires?"

"No, Justin. This conversation has gone way off course. Your pride irritates me. But we do have business to discuss." Gerard took a sip from his brandy glass.

"You've heard about the murders that have taken place in Paris, am I right?" Gerard asked.

"I saw one of the bodies the other night down by the Seine."

50

"But you didn't see the person who committed the crime?"

"The vampire was long gone. I couldn't even pick up any of the vampire's scent, although the poor woman hadn't been dead for very long."

"You didn't pick up the scent of a vampire because I believe that a mortal is doing the killing. There are a handful of mortals who have dealings with vampires. I think one of these mortals had a bad experience with a vampire and is now trying to force the police into acknowledging the vampire's existence. He wants perhaps a vigilante mob to hunt us down."

"I don't see anything wrong with that."

"Justin, what if Madeline is now a vampire?"

"I would have to destroy her, as I attempted to do with my mother."

"Attempted means you didn't have the stomach to complete the staking."

"I staked her, but I left her body whole, and another vampire now walks in her flesh."

Gerard gulped down the rest of the brandy.

"You are a very serious young man. Okay, let's forget about my trying to talk you into righting a wrong against vampires. Oh, Justin, please don't cringe at my words. It makes me feel uncomfortable to be sitting here with you."

"Is everything all right?" the waitress asked. "Is your hand still bleeding? I'd still be willing to drive you to the emergency room."

"No, I'm fine. See, there's only a small amount of

blood on the bandage, and that occurred when you first wrapped my hand."

"Good. You had me and the owner worried."

"The owner?"

"Stephan, behind the bar." She leaned her head toward the bar. "He'd like to offer this table another round of drinks."

"Wonderful idea, mademoiselle. Drink up, Justin, don't fall behind."

Justin hadn't even touched the glass in front of him.

"I'll bring another brandy for you, monsieur. And if you'd like another beer, please let me know," she said to Justin.

"I think I've had enough," he said, raising his bandaged hand to her.

She smiled at Justin and moved on to another table.

"I want you to find the person who is draining the victims' blood. And when you do, destroy him. In return, I'll give you instructions on how to get to a brothel Sade likes to visit," said Gerard.

"Where is this brothel?"

"In one of the worst parts of Paris, but that shouldn't put you off. This particular brothel pays for imported sex slaves, and the owner doesn't care about how young the slaves are."

"I don't know who is doing the killings. Perhaps the killer is a vampire. Have you considered that? Look at Marissa. She had no compunction about murdering mortals. Maybe the murders will stop now that you've destroyed her."

"No, too sophisticated to be Marissa. Besides, she wouldn't have wanted the police on her trail. I'm certain the murderer is a mortal. The bodies are being dumped in public places," said Gerard.

"I need to find Madeline now, not after I've searched out this phantom mortal you're talking about."

"I'll give you the information to find Sade tonight and will accept your word that you will also look for the murderer."

"What if I never find the killer?"

"I know you'll stick by your word and try. If you can't locate the murderer, I'll believe you."

"A brandy for monsieur." The waitress placed the balloon glass on the table and turned to Justin. "Are you sure I can't get something else for you?"

Justin rudely waved her away.

"Be kinder, Justin. I think she's interested in you. Haven't you noticed the way her face reddens when you look at her?"

"She is not Madeline."

"The one you love cannot always be at your side. Take comfort from other arms when they are offered."

"You have a deal, Gerard. I will look for the killer, but you must first tell me how to find Sade."

THIRTEEN

The bodies of the mother and son were found in an alleyway. Both had jagged cuts in their throats and both were practically empty of blood.

"But, monsieur, why would you send your son out to get his mother? Why not simply call her sister?"

"Because she could have ignored the telephone call. Her son she couldn't ignore."

"Where had you been prior to finding the bodies?"

"At home."

"Alone?"

"No, I was with my daughter. Thank God I hadn't sent them both."

"I'm surprised you didn't send your daughter to look for both of them, monsieur."

The father heard the sarcasm in the detective's voice.

"It was too late to send her. It was only six o'clock when I sent my son. He's often out later than that."

"What made you look in the alley, monsieur?"

The father's body shivered in the hot room. Most of the detectives worked with rolled-up shirtsleeves.

"Would you like some coffee, perhaps?"

The father shook his head wildly before tipping back his head to keen loudly.

He felt a paper cup being pressed into his right hand, and he gripped it so tightly that the water over-flowed onto his trousers.

"Monsieur, you understand the importance of our getting as much information as we can about your fam-ily's death. As much as we understand the pain you feel, we cannot let the perpetrator move too far ahead of us."

Someone took the shriveled cup from his hand. He looked down at his lap and immediately became em-barrassed when he saw the wetness of his trousers' crotch. Had he peed himself? He crossed his hands in front of himself to hide the water stain.

"Here are some towels, monsieur. It is only water and won't leave a stain."

He remembered the cup and took the towels to dab at his trousers.

Someone pulled up a chair and sat in front of him.

"Monsieur, we don't want to keep you here all night. I'm sure you are tired, and you have a daughter waiting at home who must be very confused by now. Try to calm yourself."

The father sucked in several breaths. He envisioned his daughter. She must be wondering why he and her brother and mother haven't come home yet. He had called a neighbor who had agreed to keep his daughter for the night. But she must lie awake thinking . . . How will he tell her?

"Monsieur, why did you look in the alley?"

"Instinct. They called to me."

"Called to you, monsieur? Were they still alive?"

"No, no, they were both cold. Like ice. I just knew they were there. I faltered. I didn't want to find them, not dead. I had a small flashlight. My son had given it to me for Christmas, for my birthday, I don't know which. The light shined on his face first. He looked like he might have been crying before he was . . ."

Someone rested a hand on his left shoulder.

"His mother lay beneath him, her skirt hiked up around her waist and her panties ripped."

"There's no sign she was raped, monsieur."

"But . . ."

"Your son . . . Or someone must have interrupted."

"Oh, my God! My son may have caught the bastard in the act." He looked from one detective's face to another, wanting to know the answer.

"Or, monsieur, someone wanted us to think there was an attempted rape." The detective who spoke looked directly into the father's eyes.

"You think I may have killed them. I'm suspect because I found them? Because I'm related to them?"

Fourteen

The woman began to move around the furniture in the conservatory. She knew exactly where she wanted to place her recently purchased statue; perhaps some of the furniture might have to go.

The statue's facial resemblance was uncanny. The body, though, was more of a kind a man would dream up rather than copy. During the day, sunlight could spray a spotlight on the statue. In the evening, she could adjust the ceiling light.

She wondered whether she had done the right thing in purchasing the statue. Then again, men never paid much attention to details. Sade would be too caught up in the shape and size of the breasts to look closely at the face.

Had Justin seen the statue? Jacques had said that only she and he had viewed the statue, but then she never trusted Jacques. He could be too obsequious.

Anyway, what the hell was Justin doing at Jacques's studio? Just when she thought she had escaped the psycho, he shows up again. Why couldn't he just return to that awful New Orleans? He was suited to live in just such a place.

And then for him to make such a scene at the club. Thank goodness she had been hidden from view. Maybe Gerard finished him off. Then again, Marissa would have been more likely to do that, and word was out that Gerard had ripped her heart out. Impetuous Gerard. But that same impetuousness had filled a few of her nights with overwhelming pleasure.

She slipped onto a lounge chair to reminisce.

FIFTEEN

Justin stood at the cross streets of the Boulevards de Clichy and de Rochechouart. Sex shops and sex shows dotted the four corners of the boulevard. Prostitutes leaned against glass windows and paced the sidewalks. Occasionally, taxicabs would drop off customers at the few new trendy clubs and bars that had recently opened. At one time, Pigalle suited only the people seeking raunchy entertainment, but gentrification had begun to make inroads.

"Oh, you're too cute to spend the evening alone, monsieur." A woman approached Justin.

"I'm not interested," he said, turning away from her. He heard a burst of laughter.

"Melanie, he thinks you're a hooker. He doesn't realize that you just want him to join us for an evening at the club."

"Maybe he's right and you're wrong," she saucily answered her friend.

He heard more laughter as he hurried down the street. Finally, at the end of the block, he took a right on a narrow street that seemed to lead to a working-class neighborhood. He began to check the numbers on the houses.

He noticed that most homes were dark. He guessed that many families were in bed, needing to get some sleep before rushing to school or work.

Candlelight dimly lit the first-floor window of one Victorian house. Filmy lace curtains covered the window. A shadow moved briefly inside the room, then quickly disappeared.

He checked the address. It was the same one given him by Gerard.

Four steps led up to the front door. He had a choice of using a silver knocker in the shape of a lion's head or of pressing a lighted button to the left of the door. Before he could do either, the door opened.

A man in a very expensive wool suit almost smashed directly into Justin.

"Excuse me, monsieur. I didn't realize you were standing here." He held the door open for Justin, who thanked the man and proceeded to enter. He let the door slam closed behind him.

An ornate chandelier lit the entryway, making the marble floors sparkle and the oak walls and staircase shine. To his left and right were sliding doors etched in fine designs. A thick cranberry wool runner covered the stairway steps. No artwork hung on the walls, which were covered with a stripe wallpaper matching the color of the runner.

He heard some noise coming from under the staircase and moved forward to check. The basement door stood ajar. Two men exited quickly.

"Jean, give her time."

"But she's been here over a month. We should be . . ."

Their conversation ended when Justin came into view.

"Monsieur, how did you get in? We always keep the door locked."

"But you don't see your customers out," Justin replied.

"True. We often are remiss in that. But the door locks automatically."

"Your last customer was kind enough to hold the door for me."

One of the men stood at most four feet eleven inches. His fingers tattooed against the satin strip of his tuxedo pants. The man next to him stood taller and wore a formal black suit, making him look like a funeral director. He leaned in toward the shorter man to whisper.

"A client. He doesn't look like a client, Robert. Look at what he is wearing. We don't cater to his kind. Go back to Pigalle, monsieur, the whores await you," the shorter man said.

"I'm a friend of Sade's," Justin stated.

"He might be, Martin. What if he is? We could be in a lot of trouble if we snubbed a friend of Sade's."

61

"Martin, I hope your height doesn't reflect the size of your brain." Justin's voice held menace.

"You have money, then?" Martin asked.

"I don't need money."

Robert began to laugh.

"Martin, we should give him some credit for being so brazen."

"He gets no credit here." Martin's lips tightened, his cheekbones became more pronounced, and his eyebrows sank down low, almost touching his eyelids.

Justin searched his pockets. He knew he didn't have enough money to satisfy these two men.

"I like him."

"What?" Martin asked, turning to his partner. "Like him? You don't even know him. He obviously is making up this relationship with Sade."

"How would he know that Sade comes here?"

"And that he has been here recently," Justin said, hoping this was true.

Martin glanced at Justin, perturbed by his own doubts.

Robert beckoned Justin to follow him. Robert opened a broad set of double doors, revealing a warmly lit room filled with bookshelves, all completely filled. Leather chairs were scattered randomly throughout the room. Straight ahead stood a bartender dressed in a tuxedo that duplicated Martin's. His hand rested on an oak bar on which a number of crystal decanters sat.

"What is your preference? Blondes, brunettes, redheads? Ah, I see a spark of life flicker in you, monsieur, at the word 'redheads.' *Oui?*"

"*Oui.* Do you have a redhead?"

"Male? Female? What is your pleasure this night?"

"Female."

"Age?"

"What the hell are you doing?" Martin had joined them at the threshold.

"I'll not have Sade snubbing us because of your idiotic suspicions. We can safely say we met his friend . . . What is your name, monsieur?"

"Justin."

"You have no father," Martin yelled.

Robert smiled.

"We are very discreet. Certainly, Sade has told you that. But we do like to know the full names of our clients in case . . ." He looked at his partner.

"You pay for what you damage, monsieur," Martin clarified.

Robert eagerly nodded his head. With an obnoxious smirk he said, "Sade definitely knows of our policy."

"Then let him be responsible for what I do." Justin hoped his defiance would hold the men at bay. He felt the little man creep up on him.

"A drink," shouted Robert. "We should share a drink together. Arno, Martin and I will have our usuals, and Justin will have . . ."

"Blood." Unsure of why he said the word, Justin moved into the room to hide his confusion.

63

"But that is precious, Justin. For that one must pay up front," Robert said.

"But it can be gotten." Justin waited a few seconds for an answer. He heard the two men behind him argue in muffled tones. Meanwhile, Arno stood at attention waiting for Justin's order.

"I can't, damn it." Martin pulled Justin around to face him. "Who are you? How do you know Sade?"

"We share a woman," Justin said.

"Not anyone who works here."

"She had better not be."

"We want nothing to do with lovers' quarrels." Robert stepped forward to speak.

"You realize that Sade is capable of killing you. We could give him your description and he would seek you out."

"I am looking for him."

"Not here." The partners spoke in sync.

"When do you expect him again?"

The men looked at each other. Obviously, an appointment had been made.

"I will lurk outside this house until he comes. If the police haven't noticed this place, they will. If you pay them protection money, it will increase."

Martin's breathing became ragged, and Robert made a hand movement toward the bartender. Immediately, Justin heard the clink of glasses and the gurgle of alcohol being poured.

"There's a boy—"

"Shut up, Robert."

"Young. We judge him to be fourteen, fifteen tops. He is upstairs now, waiting for Sade to take him home. The boy has nowhere else to go. Certainly, we can't see him go to one of those filthy orphanages or delinquent homes."

"How generous of you," Justin whispered.

"We have been feeding him. Bought him one or two outfits. But he doesn't belong with us. Not the kind of business we are in."

"And what does Sade want with the boy?"

Robert shrugged.

"What is Sade paying you?"

"Enough to cover expenses and a bit extra for our thoughtfulness."

The bartender arrived with two drinks on a tray. Robert took both and handed one to Martin.

"You need this for your nerves, I'm sure."

Martin swallowed the amber liquid in two swallows. Robert sipped his while quietly watching Justin.

"I want to see the boy."

"The boy is valuable."

"He's not chattel."

Martin smashed his glass against the marble fireplace.

Robert flinched but didn't bother to look at his partner.

"Justin . . ." Robert attempted to put his arm around Justin's shoulder, but Martin pushed his arm away.

"What game are you playing, Robert?" Martin turned to the bartender and said, "Throw this asshole out!"

Sixteen

"Watch, watch. Careful." Jacques hated delivering his sculpted Madeline to the client. He wanted a few more days to caress the smoothness of her form, touch the fullness of her lips, and contemplate the possibility that she might return for one more lesson completely cured of her old love affair.

"Stop," he shouted.

The men he usually hired had not been available. The client had refused to wait and had sent her own men. Beasts, he thought. Pale, gawky zombies that obviously knew nothing about art. If this represented a hint of how she would care for his statue, perhaps he should return the money to her. She didn't deserve his treasure. Only, she had paid a fortune, more than he had ever gotten for one of his pieces.

"Maybe if you allowed me to help," he suggested.

"Hell, you can carry it all on your back if you want," the skeletal zombie said.

"How do you know madame?" he asked.

"She's our mistress."

"You are her servants, then?"

"If you make us hang around any longer, you'll find out what we are." The strange man licked his lips.

"I'm sure she wouldn't be happy if you delivered a damaged statue."

"We know what we're doing," one of the other zombies said. "Don't irritate François."

I doubt it, Jacques thought, but instead of making war he simply threw up his hands and allowed them to proceed down the long staircase of his building.

He noted that the men had no trouble carrying the statue. No, what worried Jacques was how nonchalantly they did it. He kept wanting to tell them about the many hours he had spent on the statue and how much their "mistress" had paid. Yet he didn't. He felt they were too stupid to understand, too uneducated in the arts, too careless, and most of all, too ominous.

The one that had licked his fat lips kept looking back at Jacques, daring the artist to say something, eyeing him as if he were dinner. *Yes, that's it,* Jacques thought. The man had a hungry look. Not because of his thinness, but because of the flicker in his eyes. His glances at Jacques could almost be called lewd.

Sorry, fellow, you are just not my type.

Finally, they had made it down to street level. He saw a rented truck in front of the door.

"You can't just load it on that truck. You must crate it. Otherwise, it will arrive in a million pieces."

"François will be riding in the back with it." The zombie who spoke nodded his head to the hungry one, who smiled broadly at Jacques.

"You can ride in the back with me if you'd like," he suggested.

Before Jacques could answer, one of the other zombies spoke. "He stays behind."

Shocked, Jacques began to shake his head.

"No, no. I always accompany my work. I must find the best place for it."

"Maîtresse will know."

"Only the artist can truly relate to his work. I know what the statue means."

"Yeah, you were having too many wet dreams," François said. "Let him ride with me."

The zombie who seemed to be in charge shook his head. "What do we do with him at the end?"

"I can take a taxi," Jacques offered.

"You had the last one," François sulkily complained.

"The last what?" asked Jacques, remembering the leer that had been in François's eyes. Perhaps he needn't place the statue tonight. He could call the client tomorrow and offer to come over.

The zombielike men resumed loading the statue without crating it first. He watched François lick his lips and fondle the coolness of the statue. Once the statue had been loaded, two of the zombies returned to the cab of the truck.

"Come on. We can't keep Maîtresse waiting,"

François said, waving his hand toward where the statue sat on the truck.

Jacques hated this. He knew his Madeline needed him. She depended on him to place her in just the right light, not too near radiating heat, a stable place where she couldn't be knocked over.

"I'll call madame tomorrow," Jacques said, reluctantly moving away from the truck.

Jacques could have sworn that he heard François hiss and flash sharp, pointy teeth, but then it may have been a trick of the streetlights and the steam from some vent. In a flash, François disappeared inside the truck and pulled the door down.

The truck pulled away and Jacques almost thought he felt tears come to his eyes. Almost—except he didn't know how to cry.

SEVENTEEN

"No, Martin. My gut tells me that Justin will not leave quietly, and if we have a brawl on our steps, it will chase away our clients. Justin seems to suspect that we may even be harboring the young woman he is looking for." Robert turned toward Justin. "Am I right?"

"You said you had redheads," said Justin.

"Not real redheads. They're hard to come by. We have a few women shave their snatches and dye their hair. Most of our clients are happy with the charade."

"Why are we wasting our time with this asshole?" Martin asked.

"We have nothing to hide, Martin. Justin doesn't care about our business. He just wants to assure himself that his lover doesn't work here. Isn't that true, Justin?"

Several seconds passed and no one spoke. Only a slight clink could be heard as the bartender put away the bottles he had been using.

"There's your answer, Robert," Martin chided. "I

don't propose throwing him out. Taking his life is more my idea. He's a bum. Look at how carelessly he dresses. Certainly, Sade would have no interest in this garbage."

"I believe him, Martin. He knows Sade. They may not be best friends, but . . ."

Justin turned to exit the room.

Robert and Martin hoped Justin had decided to leave, but the bartender, having spent many years as a bouncer, knew better and chased after Justin.

Justin placed his right foot on the first step of the broad staircase when the bartender grabbed hold of both his arms. Justin found himself whirled 180 degrees and flung across the hall.

"How is that, Robert? Your gut tell you anything else about this shit who wants to invade the privacy of our club?" Martin asked.

Justin faced the three men. His flesh burned, his eyes ached, and the shading of the men's flesh seemed tinged with a wrathful green. His appearance must have altered, because both Robert and Martin stepped back into the parlor, leaving the bartender alone in the hall.

Justin wanted to tell the bartender to get out of the way. He wanted to demand free access to the entire brothel. He could not find the words.

Warily, the bartender approached Justin, the bartender's steps skittish and his breath hesitant with the doubts obviously passing through his brain.

Justin grabbed the bartender's tuxedo jacket, hearing the lapels partially rip. The man's hands swatted at

Justin's fists but he couldn't tear himself free; he dug his manicured fingernails into Justin's flesh, scraping and clawing like a woman.

Justin became aware of a hunger that he had rarely felt before, a blood hunger that he had experienced only in the midst of sexual passion. The bartender's jugular appeared to beat hard enough to make his flesh throb noticeably. The taste of blood lay heavy on Justin's dry tongue.

The bartender beat Justin about the face and upper body, but the blows seemed empty of any real force. Justin's eyes fixed on the bartender's flushed skin, the perspiration glistening under the light of the hall chandelier, the distorted features with the mouth heaving hot waves of a repulsive sour odor.

The room went dark, but Justin's eyes could still see the raw, red flesh of his prey. A scream came from the staircase, a woman sounding hysterical.

In the confusion Justin lost his hold on the bartender, who almost lost his footing but righted himself in time to step out of Justin's way.

Justin touched the banister and slowly took each step, moving closer to the female. Midway up the staircase, Justin faced a crying black woman with tattoos etched on her cheeks and forehead. Her naked body, slim but with pendulous breasts, shook violently. His hands circled her upper arms easily, the bones and tendons near the surface of her flesh.

"What happened to you?" he softly asked. But when she looked at him, her wild eyes didn't seem able to focus on his face. "Turn the lights back on," he shouted.

Almost immediately, the chandelier lit up.

"What the hell are you doing, Robert?" raged Martin at the foot of the staircase.

Robert bounded up the staircase to stand next to Justin.

"This isn't the way it should be," said Robert. "Our merchan—I mean our employees are important to us. He didn't pay for anything more than a fuck."

Justin looked down at her body and saw blood spilling down her thighs. Large clots stuck to her inner thighs, and he could see her weakening, almost ready to collapse.

Justin raised his right arm, sending Robert tumbling down the stairs.

"I'll take you out of here," Justin said to her.

She sank down, and Justin gently lowered her onto one of the steps. A film settled over her eyes, taking away the fright, replacing it with acceptance. Suddenly, she saw him and reached a hand up to touch his face.

"I'll get you out of here," he promised.

She spoke words that he could not understand, and by the sound of her voice he knew she would die.

He heard steps move down the staircase, closing in. Seconds later, euro bills rained down upon them.

"That's for the inconvenience I may have caused the house, but I know you people know how to deal with these matters. I just got carried away."

The woman's hand left Justin's face to reach for one

of the banknotes. The woman weighed the worth of her life between her fingers before collapsing into death.

Justin found himself alone on the staircase, realizing that the man who had done this must be almost at the door. He let go of the woman's body and raced down the steps to find the man dead on the hallway floor. Martin stood next to the body, gun in hand and silencer in place.

"Nobody cheats us. She was worth more than he could ever afford," Martin stated, looking at Justin and raising the gun.

"Wait," Robert commanded, still lying on the cold floor. "He's not an ordinary man. You saw him with Arno."

"I saw Arno lose his nerve."

"And it was the first time Arno ever lost his nerve. Why, Arno? Tell Martin why."

"He's not mortal," said Arno. "I used all my strength, but it meant nothing to him. I don't think he's mortal."

"I can check that out right now." Martin smirked, taking aim.

Quickly, Robert jumped up and knocked the gun from Martin's hand.

"What if that bullet didn't kill him? It would give him cause to kill us all."

"Okay, do you have a stake handy?"

"Martin, don't play with these creatures. Let's give him what he wants and be rid of him." Robert turned to

Justin. "You're looking for a woman. What's her name?"

"Madeline." Justin took a photo of her out of his pocket and handed it to Robert.

"Never seen her."

Justin made a move toward Robert, who quickly raised his hands.

"After all that has happened tonight, I wouldn't lie to you. I'd rather give you the woman and be free of you, but we don't have her. Sade doesn't supply us with people. It's the opposite."

"The boy you spoke of earlier."

"Yes, we're going to give him to Sade."

"When?"

Robert looked at Martin, who shrugged his shoulders.

"We don't know yet," said Robert. "He doesn't always call ahead. I believe he doesn't completely trust us."

"And you're asking me to?"

"No, I want you to use common sense. Our business has been completely disrupted since you walked in the door. Personally, I'd give you anything you wanted in order to see you leave."

"Give me the boy that Sade wants."

"Shit, you can't pay us anywhere near what Sade shelled out," blurted Martin.

"I don't plan on paying you anything."

Robert commanded Arno to fetch the boy.

"Sade's going to expect to get his money back," Martin complained.

"And we can afford to reimburse him. One less million for each of us.

"We have a big cleanup job, Justin. I hope when Arno brings the boy you won't linger."

Hearing a skirmish behind him, Justin turned to see Arno dragging a youth down the steps. The boy appeared to be barely fourteen. His blue-black hair was kinked into luscious curls that almost reached the collar of his shirt. His fair eyes made Justin think that the boy's olive skin was tanned darker than its usual color. His sullen features and gawky movements implied that he had not been enjoying his stay in the brothel.

"Robert, what will we tell Sade?" asked Martin.

Robert looked toward Justin, who pulled a paper and pen from the pocket of his jeans and quickly wrote his name and address.

"Tell Sade that I have the boy," Justin said, handing the sheet of paper to Robert.

Eighteen

"Madame, I am so sorry. I normally would never have let a delivery be made without my being present. I take great pride in my work and make sure it is placed appropriately in the home of my patrons." Sounding both unctuous and prideful, Jacques begged his mysterious client to forgive his inability to accompany his statue of Madeline.

"Not to worry, Jacques. My sense of beauty is impeccable, and I've placed your work in a better place than even you would have been able to. Seems one of my workers was upset, though. He took a shine to you, monsieur, and to be honest, that isn't good."

"You mean the one the others called François?"

"Exactly. He apparently covets your . . ." The client hesitated for several seconds. "Never mind. Doesn't matter. You and he will probably not have another occasion to meet."

"I'll be sure my men are available for delivery next time, madame."

"Next time? You've rooked me once with your high prices, Jacques—are you trying to drive me into the poorhouse?"

"Madame, the statue is worth every euro you paid for it. If you are not satisfied, I am willing to take it back and return your money. I want my work to sit in the home of someone who recognizes fine art."

"Don't be insulted, Jacques. I want to keep the statue."

Jacques sighed with relief. He had already spent the money, and there wasn't a long line of art collectors waiting outside his door.

"Matter of fact, I might want to have an image of myself sculpted."

"I would be pleased to do so, madame." Jacques had no idea what his client looked like. She had always appeared draped in dark, heavy cloth, with an almost opaque veil over her face.

"Must you skim the model's body with your hands?"

"Not necessarily. I did the statue you bought from my imagination."

"Pity. I would rather have every curve reflect my true body."

Jacques had never played at being a gigolo, but he sensed the opportunity was becoming available.

"Of course, madame is right. Touching the flesh always enhances the final work."

"With the use of all your senses you could compose a duplicate of your model."

"There is nothing, madame, like flesh. The clay is a poor imitation of a woman's softness and receptiveness."

"Ah, receptiveness is only a reflection of a man's skill."

"As you can tell, madame, I have no doubts about mine."

"Someday you must come over and give proof of your boastful claim."

Fearing he would lose his tenuous hold on madame's checkbook, Jacques dared to suggest a possible date and time for a meeting.

The client laughed and asked, "Shall I send François to pick you up?"

"I have been living in Paris for many years, madame. I know the city extremely well. A simple address is all I need."

"But François would be upset if he weren't here to at least greet you, monsieur. I treasure François and wouldn't want him to hand in a pouty resignation."

"I'm sure there are many who could take his place."

"Would you be willing to take his place?"

"That kind of manual labor would waste my talents."

"His job isn't just to act as a delivery person, monsieur. He, too, has talents."

Jacques figured that this woman had tested all of François's talents.

"A pity, madame, that you can't find the time to pose. Remember, beauty is not timeless."

"Unless carved in clay."

"Even then, slight chips or careless scratches can wear away the beauty of the artwork."

"How grave your are, monsieur, and how depressing. François never worries about such things."

"That's why he loads statutes onto trucks and I sculpt them."

"I'll tell François what you said. Perhaps that will encourage him to sign up for your classes. Good night, monsieur."

Nineteen

What a horror of a woman, Jacques thought, relieved that she had rejected his offer. And if that François ever showed up at the door, Jacques would immediately call the gendarmes.

The door buzzer sounded, and Jacques nearly dropped the telephone.

Nonsense, Jacques realized, François couldn't possibly have overheard the conversation, and if he had, there is no way he could have arrived so quickly at the front door.

He placed the phone back on the marble-topped table and padded barefoot to the front door. With bravado Jacques pulled open the door.

"Madeline!"

"Jacques, may I come in?"

"Why not, my love."

Dressed in an oversized man's shirt and very tight

jeans, she looked inviting. She obviously had bunched her hair atop her head to get it out of the way. A tortoiseshell comb barely kept the strands of hair from falling into her face.

"I was worried that I might not see you again. The young man with whom you had been living paid me a visit."

"Justin. He must be angry."

"Worried. I don't think he's been able to reach deep enough inside himself to find the anger."

Madeline sat on the sofa, a perturbed expression marring the beautiful features.

"It is certainly none of my business why you two broke up. I'm just glad you've decided to continue your lessons."

"Oh, no, I can't. I would never be able to concentrate."

"Because of Justin?"

"No. You must tell Justin that I didn't mean to hurt him."

"I don't have any rapport with your boyfriend, my love. Besides I would be suspect all over again if I were to admit seeing you."

"But I need your help."

"Has Justin ever hurt you?"

"No. He is sweet."

"I guess one would have to be female to see how 'sweet' he is. But you do seem fearful of something."

"I need money."

"So why come here?"

"You've been filling up all your time with students

to teach and works that you've been selling. I thought you wouldn't mind helping us."

"You and Justin?"

"No. Please, a small amount would help. We need to get off the streets."

"You're living on the streets? I must say this new boyfriend doesn't seem to be an improvement. Justin may be a bore, but he kept you housed and fed. Why not go back to him?"

"Because I know what he'd do if . . ."

"He would welcome you with open arms, as far as I can tell."

"But not the person I'm with."

"You ask a lot of a man, my love. Even I might be willing to allow you to stay here, but certainly not when you drag around a leech such as you've found."

"I didn't ask you to get involved. I only wanted some money."

"Did you expect charity, or did you plan on paying it back with interest?"

"I didn't get any further than to hope you could spare me something. I don't know when I shall be able to pay you back. I don't even know whether he and I will survive."

Jacques sat down on the sofa next to her.

"Madeline, a woman of your beauty need not keep a man."

"I'm not keeping him, Jacques." Anger made her voice rise. "I am taking care of someone very important to me."

"Explain the difference, my love."

Madeline got to her feet.

"Leaving is not going to solve your problem, Madeline. You are not the only woman who has fallen in love with a wastrel."

Madeline started for the door.

"I didn't say I wouldn't give you any money. I simply asked how you would pay it back."

TWENTY

Justin sat in the old rocker, staring at the boy sleeping in his bed. He'd been sleeping over ten hours and showed no sign of waking. Several times he had squirmed in his sleep and uttered indecipherable sounds. Once he even seemed to be beating up his pillow, his fists moving in quick, short bursts of energy.

Neither had spoken to each other all the way back to the garret. The boy had refused the bed until he understood that Justin would be sleeping in the rocker. And Justin's back ached now in complaint.

"Mama," the boy shouted, sitting bolt upright on the mattress. "Mama," he shouted again, waiting for soft hands to push back his tight locks of hair.

Finally, the boy looked about the room, his glance falling last on Justin. The boy's lower lip extended into a pout. His dark eyebrows hovered low over his pale eyes. The boy's clothes were new and fashionable. Justin assumed Robert and Martin had seen to that.

"I'm Justin. I've been told to call you Stephan. Is that really your name?"

The boy shook his head.

"Would you like to tell me your name?"

The boy shook his head.

"Are you hungry?"

The boy made no movement.

"There is food in the refrigerator. Take anything you want."

The boy still did not move.

"Robert made it clear that you do not originally come from France but do understand French."

"My nana taught me," the boy replied tersely.

"And where are you from?"

The boy hid behind his silence once again.

"Would you like to be returned home?"

"My parents are dead. My uncles sold me."

"To Robert and Martin?"

The boy shook his head.

"To someone else, who then sold you to Robert and Martin?"

"I don't know how many times I was sold. The men were all different and foreign. Most kept me shackled and barely fed. The two men at that house locked me in a room but didn't burn my wrists with their irons." The boy exposed his wrists, which were rubbed raw. "They fed me when I was hungry and gave me new clothes to wear."

"But you still didn't like them."

"They still took away my freedom. They said a man would come for me."

"Not me. No. I was looking for someone else. I can't claim to be better than any of the other men you've met on your journey. I use you now as bait."

"You want to find my new jailor."

"I'll not give you to him, though."

"You'll keep me for yourself."

"No. I'm not sure what to do with you. Drop you off at Social Services or at the commissariat, I guess."

"And they'll throw me into a new jail."

"No, they'll find your family." Justin realized his words were no comfort. "You'll probably be sent back at least to the country you come from."

"The Ukraine."

Justin knew the boy's life wouldn't get any better there. The boy was too old for adoption and had no relatives in France. He'd be left to roam the streets of his homeland until death found him.

"Let me prepare something for you to eat. I don't have much." He opened the fridge and sensed movement behind him. "If you run away from me, where will you go? Back to the brothel? Or perhaps you'll turn yourself in to the gendarmes." He turned his head toward the boy. "Are you in a hurry to go home?"

TWENTY-ONE

"Marie, why are you giggling to yourself like a crazy woman?" asked Sade.

"Artists are such sensitive souls. So easy to manipulate and tease."

"Client or lover?" he asked.

"Right now I'm his client, but that could change. I may even be able to get back quite a bit of the money I paid him."

In the middle of the room, Sade kicked off his shoes and headed toward the bookcase.

"You are a slob, Louis."

Sade managed to ignore Marie while he searched the shelves for a decent book to read.

"Have you been in the salon today, Louis?"

"Since you seem interested in calling that room to my attention, I'll make sure to avoid it." Sade slipped one of the old, leather-bound books off a shelf.

"I wish you wouldn't insist on being contrary. Perhaps there's a wonderful surprise waiting for you."

"Not wonderful if you put it there." He started to leave but stopped on the room's threshold. "Does this have anything to do with François and the other buffoons you created?"

Marie gave him a sly smile.

"I was wondering why those horrors were wandering around here. I wish you'd keep your feeble attempts at starting a clan far away from this residence or move out."

"Lilliana would never allow you to force me out."

"She is the only reason you're here." He nodded.

Marie stood and stroked her Lycra-covered hips with the palms of her hands.

"Sure it isn't my body?"

"You disgust me, Marie." He almost turned to go, but she saw him stop with a worried look on his face. "What's in the salon, Marie?"

"I couldn't decide whether to purchase it, except Jacques had done such a wondrous job that I couldn't resist. I was going to be silent about it, though, and hope you wouldn't notice anything special about it except the beauty of the piece."

"Jacques. He is the sculptor you've been talking about?"

She nodded excitely.

"You must see it." She merrily wiggled her hips, crossed the room, and took Sade's arm. Before he could protest, she dragged him down the hall, releasing his arm only when she flung the double doors to the salon open.

The book slipped from Sade's hand and bounced on the marble floor. The fall dented the edge of the binding.

"Who the hell's body did he give her?" Sade yelled out.

Marie glanced in at the statue of Madeline.

"Her own, I assumed."

Sade walked into the salon and circled the statue.

"These are Madeline's features," he said, waving his hand toward the face of the statue. "But certainly the hips are much too broad, and the body is deformed in comparison to Madeline's. He's ruined her beauty for the rest of eternity."

"Don't be so dramatic, Louis. Just say you don't find the statue to be exact enough. Her own beauty is going to fade within the next few years. Probably someday she'll wistfully stare at what Jacques has produced."

"One hopes she'll never see it. She certainly didn't pose for this."

"No, I guess she's too demure."

"How did he meet her? Is she in Paris?"

"Your eyes sparkle too much when you speak of her, Louis. From what I've heard, she's been living with Justin here in Paris." Marie felt satisfied that the mention of Justin quickly dulled Sade's eyes. "I've seen him around, by the way. Evidently, your sweet little Madeline has been taking art classes with Jacques. Using her warm, delicate fingers to sculpt artwork of her own." Marie spread her own fingers over Sade's hips. "But you would know how talented she is with her fingers, I suppose."

Sade pried each of Marie's fingers from his body, finally casting aside Marie's hands as if they were contaminated.

"She's missing, Louis, and there is talk that she may be with you. At least that's what Justin believes."

"Therefore, you had to buy this statue to stoke the rumors."

"No, Louis. I fell in love with the statue before Madeline went missing. Although I did find the situation amusing. That's why I had François and the others pick up the statue. The incompetent Jacques couldn't get his own staff together on time. I think François has a bit of a thing for Jacques."

"Of course he does. Jacques has warm blood, doesn't he?"

"I wish you'd be kinder to my flock, Louis."

"Flock? Are you a priestess or minister now? Hell, I need a diversion from this chicanery you've begun."

TWENTY-TWO

Justin entered the café from the rear door, not wanting to be seen first. He immediately spied Gerard staring out the window at a front table.

The vampire tapped his glossy, finely manicured nails on the white tablecloth. He had the day's newspaper resting beside a large, white cup. His clothes were immaculate, the colors all matched, and not a wrinkle marred the folds of his garments.

Justin walked to the table and sat down in the chair opposite Gerard, who had just lifted his cup.

"Ah, Justin, I'm glad you made it." Gerard started to take a sip and realized the cup was empty. "I must order another. I can never get enough of their chocolate here."

Justin noticed a light stain of chocolate above Gerard's upper lip. He liked seeing the flaw and felt his body relax.

After ordering two chocolates, Gerard turned back to Justin.

"It's my treat. I hate drinking alone, but then I rarely do." Gerard gave Justin a broad smile. "Have you found your Madeline as yet?"

"No."

"And Sade?"

"I have something he wants. He'll find me."

"Not the best way to initiate contact with him. He doesn't like being pushed around by anyone. You would do a lot better if you attempted to be civil, Justin. Your moodiness grates on most of us."

"You mean on vampires?" Justin asked.

"Thank you, mademoiselle." The waitress placed a cup in front of each of them. "I have a question to ask you, mademoiselle. You notice the young man seated at this table with me is quite good-looking. Needn't blush, mademoiselle. I do not have erotic interest in men, but even I will admit he is handsome. However, what do you think of his attitude? Do you think he is a bit moody? Dark would be a good description of the mood he projects. Not someone you'd want to spend a great amount of time with, eh?"

"Enough, Gerard. You're making her feel awkward."

"I don't mean to do that," Gerard said, taking the waitress's hand. She visibly shivered when he touched her.

"Let her be," Justin said, reaching across the table to separate Gerard from the waitress, who quickly escaped.

"The mortals are so naive, Justin. They have no idea of the power people like us share."

"I have no special powers, Gerard. I assume I will age and die like all the other mortals."

"Why do you assume that?"

"I am not a vampire."

"And you say it so confidently because you fear that you are." Gerard smiled, lifted his cup, toasted Justin, and took a sip. "You're in love with a woman and yet won't make love to her. I frighten you because I'm something that you may possibly be. Why do you destroy vampires, Justin? Is it to destroy a part of what you are? You're not on a moral crusade. No, you merely fear what you are."

Justin's flesh prickled. He tried to pick up the cup in front of him, but he noticed a slight quiver and replaced the cup on the table. He wouldn't allow Gerard to trap him into exposing anything about himself.

"Gerard, I'm here because you wanted to know whether I've discovered anything about the person committing the murders. I told you I had nothing new, and you insisted on this meeting."

"Yes, Justin. I should be more gracious. You've heard the gendarmes are holding the husband and the father of the last two victims. I think the gendarmes are grabbing at straws. Too many people have become irate over the murders, and the gendarmes are looking for an easy target. But this man is not the killer. He has no connection with the other murders."

"Is he a vampire?"

"No, very mortal."

"Doesn't he fit your profile?"

"Just being mortal is not the only criterion."

"Do you have a list?"

"No, I leave this sport to you, Justin. I'm sure you always make sure you stake vampires and not some nincompoop playacting. Did you ever worry about being wrong, Justin? Has there been a time when you've hesitated? But of course not. Hesitation could cause your own demise. So your snap judgments must always be correct. Isn't that right, Justin?"

"You're not asking me for answers, Gerard. You read me well. Yes, I have doubts. I sometimes heave my guts up next to a vampire I destroyed. I come across children that you savages have changed. Some barely toddlers. Can you imagine not just sucking dry but actually changing a child that has barely learned to walk? Why? The little ones look at me with hunger but aren't equipped to feed. I stake them and hunt for the vampires who knowingly rob mortals of their lives."

Gerard sat back and clapped, finally settling the palms of his hands upon his knees.

"Someday you will acknowledge that you are more vampire than mortal, Justin. And certainly in no way are you God."

"You bait me and God with all your accusations."

"No, no, Justin. I'm helping you. God is the only One that has been cruel to you."

TWENTY-THREE

"We'll take Yvette home with us."

The father turned rapidly around to face his deceased wife's sister. She wore charcoal gray instead of black, and heavy evening-wear makeup. Not a single stroke of makeup had run.

"It is not necessary, Babbette. The gendarmes have set me free. I can go home now and take care of my daughter myself."

His sister-in-law stiffened.

"There will be much talk about what has happened, Jean. I am only trying to protect her from the embarrassment and chiding that her peers may cause."

"I'm sure she'll survive. Besides, I think she needs her old friends right now, not the snots that live in your part of Paris."

"Let me be honest with you. We don't trust you around Yvette."

"We who? You and the British lord you're married to?"

"Reginald and I have considered moving to England for a while. Yvette is going to need time to recuperate from the shock of losing both her mother and her brother. And no one knows if you'll stay out of jail." Her eyebrows rose slightly with her last sentence.

"I didn't kill your sister, Babbette, and I don't know how you could even suspect me of murdering my own son. When he was newborn, I worked two jobs in order to give him everything he needed. He was me. He was my life. Even you admitted that Matthew and I looked exactly alike. The poor boy even had my hammertoe. You think I raised him all these years just so I could kill him?" He realized his voice had been getting loud when he noticed sideways looks from the people around him. His daughter stood by the open grave over which the coffin sat perched, and she kept her hands clasped in prayer.

"I don't see why you should be so bitter. If you truly cared about your daughter, you'd allow me to take Yvette to England. No one there would know of all this."

"They don't read papers in England, Babbette? The newspapers are saying these killings are part of a chain of deaths. People everywhere will enjoy having their breakfast over such a story. The tabloids in England will be speculating on all sorts of schemes. My family's photographs have been passed on throughout the world."

Babbette moved closer to the father.

"You are raising your voice again. You have no self-control. Yet you expect me to leave my only niece with you."

"She is my only daughter, Babbette," he whispered.

"Even more reason to want her to be free of the carnival that will surround these killings."

"We need each other now. If you asked Yvette, she would tell you that she wanted to stay with me. When I came home from prison, she wouldn't let me out of her sight. She spent the whole night sleeping in my arms."

"How vulgar," Babbette sniped. "She is too old to be sleeping in her father's bed."

"Stay away from us, you barren whore," he shouted, turning to see his daughter staring at him with round eyes.

His heart stopped but a moment, his breath halted, and his flesh went cold. How could he apologize for his outburst? He never meant to separate Yvette from his wife's family. All he had wanted was Babbette's help, but she insisted on robbing him of his only living child.

Yvette ran to her father and threw her arms around his body. It took him several seconds before he could loosen her grip and pick her up.

The car door stood open and the driver waited patiently, attempting to ignore the family brawl that he had witnessed.

"We'll go home now, Yvette." He walked slowly, gripping his precious bundle close to him.

"In the car now." She slipped into the back seat, and he followed. The driver slammed the door and returned to the front seat.

As they pulled away from the grave, his daughter spun around on the seat to stare out the back window, catching a final glimpse of the remains of her mother and brother. He feared she would cry out and become hysterical, but instead she gave a simple wave before collapsing into her father's arms.

TWENTY-FOUR

"You knew," shouted Sade as he slammed the front door. He searched each room on the first floor until he found Marie stretched out in front of the fireplace, dipping her fingers into the creamy remains of a strawberry shortcake.

"You knew," he screamed again upon seeing her. "You knew and waited for me to find out."

"Knew what, Louis?"

"About the boy."

"Louis, I think you should try to be civil to me, at least for Lilliana's sake. We promised her that we would get along."

"No one can live with you, Marie. You are a conniving witch who can't survive without the thrill of the contest between us."

"What the hell are you accusing me of? What boy?"

"You've been to Robert's and Martin's brothel. Admit it!"

"Louis, I introduced you to the place. Have you ruined our reputations there? Can we not continue to visit that brothel? You've done something to spoil the fun we had there."

"Are you saying that you knew nothing of the agreement I had with Robert and Martin?"

"You know that I'm always very proud when I best you, Louis. I would deny nothing."

Sade slumped into a leather chair.

"How did he find out, then?"

Marie shrugged, then quizzically asked, "Who?"

"That horror you brought into my home."

"If you're talking about François . . ."

"That idiot means nothing to me."

"Do I have to spend the rest of the day going through a long list of people I know who could possibly irk you?" Marie rolled over onto her back. The frayed Persian rug on which she lay contrasted sharply with the fresh glow of her skin.

"Justin."

"Oooh!"

"After my battle with you earlier, I decided to go to the brothel and collect the child."

"How old?"

"I was told he was fourteen, fifteen. Well-educated. Talented. He played the piano, I think, or perhaps it was the flute."

"Obviously, you sought him for his musical talent." She sat up and pulled her knees close to her chest. She didn't care how much the crumpled skirt revealed.

"His parents were dead, and his family sold him into slavery, probably to keep him from inheriting his parents' property."

"I tell you, Louis, it is important to keep family together. Don't let anything like that happen to our own blood relatives."

"You are not a blood relative to me."

"I'm your child's grandmother." She smirked. "That's why I live here."

"Shut up, Marie. When I arrived at the brothel, both Robert and Martin were present. They scurried around me like frightened rats who are trapped but can't get away."

"Something's amiss, you said to yourself."

"And I was right. They explained that they no longer had the boy and the money I had paid them would be returned within the week."

"You'll never see it again unless you shake them up a bit."

"I don't care about the money, Marie. That bastard Justin has purposefully crossed my path again."

"He has the boy. What is he doing with the boy?"

"Holding him for ransom."

Marie burst out laughing.

"Justin is clever, Louis. How did he ever find out about that brothel?"

"Yes, Marie, how did he find out?"

"Not from me. I've seen him about. Once at Jacques's studio and another time at one of those clubs drifting into bankruptcy. But I never spoke to him, and

I doubt he recognized me. When I go to Jacques's, I always layer on the clothes. Somehow I don't completely trust Jacques."

Sade reached inside his coat pocket and pulled out a slip of paper.

"He left his address for me." He tossed it in her direction.

The paper landed on one of her feet, and she daintily plucked the paper up with her fingers.

"Not a very nice neighborhood," she muttered. "You suppose Madeline actually lived there with him?"

"That's her problem, not mine."

"Poor girl. You should have changed her, Louis. I think you were a fool for tossing her away."

"I have the feeling Justin thinks I came back for her. Robert and Martin babbled on about a redhead. They had no true redheads, so he took the boy instead."

"He wants an exchange."

"Except I don't have anyone to give him."

"You could let him keep the boy. I'm sure Robert and Martin could find a substitute if you gave them a few months."

Sade sat straight in his chair and intensely stared into Marie's eyes.

"This Justin has my property."

"He took Madeline, and you didn't bother to get her back."

"I was finished with Madeline. She was an idiot."

"She chose him over you, didn't she?"

"She was blinded by his sullen angst. She probably

left him when she realized there really wasn't any depth to Justin. Now he can't let go and is flailing about trying to get her back. She won't go back to him, Marie. The small amount of time she has spent with him has opened her eyes."

"Think she's looking for you?" Marie wiggled her eyebrows.

Sade got to his feet and demanded the slip of paper.

"Can I go with you?" Marie asked, handing the paper over to him.

"You still wish to view the spectacle, don't you?"

She fiercely nodded her head.

"Go get yourself a ticket to the opera, because there will be no other spectacle for you tonight."

TWENTY-FIVE

Jacques counted out the euros into Madeline's palm.

"I don't know why you look so glum, my *petite chèrie*. I have only asked you to model for me. I could have requested far more than that, and naked you certainly are enticing." He smiled and took a step closer to her.

"Remember, I am working as your model, no more than that."

"Mais oui." He gave a long, painful sigh. "And this man that you are laboring for, is he that much more handsome than I?"

"It has nothing to do with how he looks."

"Ah, then it's how he uses his . . ." Jacques reached down to touch himself.

Her eyes began to water, and Jacques stood clear of the door.

"The same time tomorrow. I'll be going out of town

for the weekend, and I'd like to finish most of the sketching by then."

Madeline gripped the money tightly and nodded her head before opening the door.

After she left, Jacques almost felt guilty, but he recalled that the little tramp had obviously chosen some scoundrel over him. *The fool,* he thought.

At least she had returned, and he could do an even better job with the next statue of Madeline.

He checked his appointment book and groaned when he saw he had no other students scheduled. Lack of money and lack of cunt would be his downfall.

The doorbell rang, and when he answered he shouted in surprise.

"Madame, nothing has happened to the statue of Madeline that I sold you, I hope."

"No, but over the phone you did seem interested in showing me more of your work and in doing a statue of me."

"Yes, yes. Come in. A drink. I have excellent brandy, but if you'd prefer a little sherry . . ."

"Blood would be nice," she responded.

Jacques hesitated a moment before deciding that she must mean wine.

"My mama always told me that red wine helps to enhance the blood, madame. I presume your mother also favored the grapes." Jacques busied himself going through the kitchen cupboards. He remembered being gifted with at least one bottle this week. His students frequently brought food or wine to suck up to him.

"You needn't bother, Jacques." She stood at the doorway to the kitchen in a stunning leather outfit, the coat, hat, and veil she had been wearing totally removed. Her plump breasts rose full-blown from above the leather barely covering her nipples.

He couldn't imagine how she had managed to corkscrew herself into the suit.

"Are you still interested in creating a statue of me, Jacques?"

"Oui!" His arms flew into the air in complete surrender.

"I suppose you're too tired to start now," she said.

"No. If you wish to begin now, I am certainly willing, except I wanted to be a good host and get you something to drink. I find many of my models relax with a touch of wine. . . ." He glanced back into one of the cupboards then back at her. "Or sherry or brandy."

"What did Madeline have?"

"I told you—she never posed for that statue. She was one of my students, not a model."

Marie tossed a sketch pad at Jacques, and when it fell to the floor he saw that it was open to the sketch he had recently completed.

"I saw her leave, Jacques. I guess you are determined to sculpt the perfect Madeline."

"The poor child needs euros. She appears to be obsessed with some good-for-nothing. The kind that needs a lot of monetary care." Jacques gave up looking for the wine and picked up his sketch pad. "She is beautiful, though. *Non?*"

"You men should form a fan club. Within the past few days, several men have raved about her beauty or taken extravagant steps to get closer to her."

Marie moved out of the kitchen, and Jacques followed closely behind while attempting to flip to a blank page.

"Certainly, she can't compete with your mature beauty, madame."

Marie stopped abruptly.

"Madeline is hardly a child. I've heard she's quite experienced."

"But you, madame, know how to dress, how to apply color to your face, how to walk so that each movement seduces, and—"

"Shut up, Jacques." She picked up her coat.

"Here, let me hang . . ." He went to take her coat, and she pulled away.

"I've become bored."

"But we haven't even started with your sketch yet."

"I wouldn't want to divert your attention from your true masterpiece. Please help me with my coat, Jacques." She handed the black camel-hair coat to him.

"Ah, madame," he said, taking her coat. "You have mature, sophisticated beauty, but you allow your youthful gremlin to sour our time with jealousy."

She slid her arms into her coat and allowed Jacques to encircle her with his arms.

"What do you feel in your arms, Jacques?"

"A beautiful woman," he breathed into her right ear.

"You feel the luxury of expensive camel hair. Far better quality than anything Madeline could afford."

"Madame, you and I know that it is not a bad thing to embrace both beauty and wealth at the same time. You do not expect money from me to support a lover, and I don't expect to have you with me for a lifetime. Each of us can cherish what the other has to offer without fretting over ridiculous fantasies." He kissed her softly on the cheek.

"I'm still a woman who needs constancy, at least while we're alone."

"I never would have shown you the sketchbook. I won't even use the same book for our sessions. But please, madame, while you are here, don't seek trouble. Don't uncover the small vices I may engage in when you are absent."

"I'll be back, Jacques."

He opened his mouth to ask a question, but before he could she placed her hand over his mouth.

"Please, Jacques, don't make demands."

He kissed the palm of her hand and allowed his eyes to smile his assent.

TWENTY-SIX

Madeline hurried down the cobblestone street clutching the bundle of used clothes she had just purchased at the charity store. A brief shower had made the cobblestones slippery, and her shoes were soaked, making it difficult for her to keep her balance. The coat she wore already had the musty smell of damp wool, and her hair drooped in strands about her face.

When she saw the door to the deserted, ramshackle house ajar, she feared that he had fled. She quickened her steps and came close to falling, except that she reached out and grabbed hold of a rusted iron fence. Her hand came away spotted with orange and black spots. Without thinking, she rubbed her hand on the thin woolen coat she wore, drying her hand before touching the doorknob. Slowly, she pushed the door all the way open, smelling the odor of spoiled food and decades of old dust.

She checked the floor for blood. Had he left to feed? Would he have dared to bring his prey back to this house?

Only green mold striped the wooden floor.

Maybe he hadn't returned as yet?

She had asked him to stay in the house. She promised not to be long, but in order to get the money she had stayed longer than expected at Jacques's studio.

The floor moaned deeply when she walked into the house. A deep moan, not a sharp squeak that one might expect. The building seemed as tired and as resigned to its fate as she and he did.

The door partially stuck when she closed it, and she had to lean her body against the door to force the lock.

On the way home, she had been in such a hurry that she hadn't noticed the cold, but now inside the abandoned house waves of chills flooded her body. Her teeth chattered, and her numb fingers almost dropped the bundle she had purchased.

Moving farther into the house, she watched her step carefully. Most of the windows had been broken, and glass covered a large part of the floors. When she first found the house, she closed and locked all the shutters, leaving the house dark and eerie, but at least no one would be able to see them moving about.

The electric did not work, but the faucet in the kitchen dripped the still-available precious water. He would huddle close to her, not against the cold but to recall the feel of body heat. Tonight she'd be unable to use her coat for warmth. She'd have to pull down some of the velvet drapes and use them as blankets. He didn't care about the cold as long as she slept next to him.

Her toes finally kicked the oil lamp that she had left on the floor. She put her bundle aside temporarily while she lit the lamp. Carrying both the lamp and the bundle, she moved to the staircase. Under the light she could see the dust that covered the banister. Here and there were prints where her or his fingers had rested, and there were smudges where one of them had grasped the banister when unsure of her or his step.

Some of the wooden steps showed splintering, and the original color of the wood bled through the old stain.

She paused a moment to listen. A sound came from the second floor, an unnatural throbbing noise that made her want to turn around and leave the house forever. But she pressed on, feeling some relief in the belief that he had stayed put. When she reached the second floor, the sounds grew louder. Quickly, she oriented herself to the direction from which the sounds came.

The peeling wallpaper curled into brittle bits of paper shaped like profiteroles, with the paste now yellow and dry. The texture embedded in the wallpaper unwound into tiny strings.

A wail called her attention away from the ruin around her and made her hurry to the doorway of what had been the master bedroom. Little luxury survived in the room. The stained silken curtains glimmered with shards of glass that had become fixed to the material. The king-size bed sloped in the direction of one missing leg, and the sheets seemed an embarrassment of faded brown stains. But he lay upon those sheets, his hands covering his face, his sobs catching in his throat, crying tearlessly.

How sad, she thought, *to weep without the release of tears.*

"I've brought some fresh clothes home. I tried to keep them dry, but the plastic bag they gave me had a few tears and . . ."

He didn't acknowledge her.

"And I'll hang them to dry along with my coat."

She dropped her bundle onto a dry washbasin that contained a cracked pitcher, as useless as she.

"Hungry," he whispered.

Not so soon, she wanted to say, but bit her tongue until she tasted blood. He wouldn't take her blood. She had offered and hoped they could modulate how much he took, but he knew better.

"Please, sweetheart, try to control the hunger. This ravenous hunger is not normal."

"It never stops," he said. "Never stops. I could kill the entire world and still it wouldn't stop. Madeline, why won't anything sate me?"

She ran to him and took him into her arms. He wrapped his arms about her, making her wet coat cling to his skin. She felt the dampness pressing through the lining, her clammy skin prickling into goose bumps.

TWENTY-SEVEN

By the time Sade arrived at Justin's garret, his anger had faded into annoyance, and he almost decided to turn back home. Almost.

Marie had been right. Other boys could be found. Besides, he had ordered up the boy as a lark. He didn't even know what the boy looked like or whether he actually was as experienced as Robert and Martin had implied. However, Sade knew Justin. Justin had stolen Madeline and now this boy.

Sade climbed the stairs, recalling the taste, smell, and feel of Madeline. Madeline, the quiet maiden that had blinded him to all the others he had bedded.

Should he kick the door in and surprise the young man, or knock civilly, hoping to contain emotions and not allow Justin the pleasure of knowing how he felt? What if Justin were not there and the boy was? Could he snatch the child away and call it even? No. The child was not the person who had brought him here.

114

He knocked softly on the door, politely. He heard the shuffle of feet coming to the door, and the boy suddenly stood before Sade. *A pretty child. Too pretty for a boy.* The wet curls and the almost feminine features made the boy look younger than his advertised age of fourteen. He wore an oversized robe that Sade assumed belonged to Justin. On the other hand, given the robe's pale color, it could have belonged to Madeline.

"Are you the man who's supposed to come for me?" the boy asked, pronouncing his words slowly.

"I'm the man who has paid for you," Sade replied, reaching out to finger the terry robe. *Cheap,* he thought.

"Justin won't let you have me."

"Has he stolen your heart too?"

The boy looked confused.

"Sade." Justin appeared suddenly from behind a screen, his clothes wrinkled, obviously from sleep.

"You can never rest when you have children. They'll open doors to complete strangers."

"Felix," Justin commanded. "Go finish dressing."

The boy hurried back into the bathroom.

"Felix? That must be the name you've baptized him with, Justin." Sade walked into the room and closed the door behind him.

"He won't tell me his name," Justin said.

"A little obstinate creature, is he?" Sade looked around for a place to sit but found the one chair piled high with clothes. "Do you expect me to sit on the floor?"

Justin brushed the clothes off the chair, spilling them onto the floor.

"Thank you." Sade checked the condition of the chair. No unusual spots. He sat. "A drink, perhaps?"

"I have nothing you'd enjoy."

"Justin, I am your guest. I would have thought you'd be ready for me. Instead the room is a hovel, the boy is rude, and you look like you haven't slept in weeks. But then, maybe you haven't. The place lacks . . . I know. The recent touch of a woman. They are good at cleaning chores, aren't they?"

"Where is she?"

"Marie? I suppose you would long to see her, since she now, to all appearances, looks like your mother. Although you didn't treat your mother well when you lived with her."

"Madeline. I want to know where Madeline is."

"The little snip that shared my bed for a short time? Certainly, you can't believe that I would have taken her back—not after the poor choice she made."

"You know where she is."

"Are you sure you don't have a bit of champagne? My favorite is Veuve Clicquot, but in a pinch I'll settle for something of lesser quality."

"That's not your favorite drink, Sade."

"There's certainly none of my favorite in this room. Unless . . ." Sade turned his head to watch the boy enter the room. "What is your real name, Felix?"

"I'm no longer who I was," the boy answered.

"Philosophical, isn't he, Justin? Have you two been

116

able to share deep conversations?" He spoke to Justin but never took his eyes off Felix.

"Forget the boy, Sade. I'd never give him to you."

"Then why waste my time?"

"He used me as bait to get you here," Felix interrupted.

"How do you feel about that, my little philosopher?" Sade asked.

"Everyone uses me now that my parents are gone."

"He'll make me weep, Justin." Sade lightly fanned his eyes.

"Tell me about Madeline."

Sade looked at Justin. "You mean what she was like in bed? But you must know that by now. Beyond that, I didn't pay much attention to her."

"I want to know where she is."

"I don't know. You've wasted your time and mine. The boy thinks we're both fools by now. I had no idea that you and Madeline were living together in Paris."

"You know now, and my guess is that you knew before you came here."

"Marie is full of information. She manages to keep track of everyone—including me, unfortunately."

Justin paced the room while the boy tried unsuccessfully to keep out of his way.

"Justin, let me invite you to my home. You can search for Madeline all you want. And we should bring the boy, for he might like living conditions better at my home."

"He stays behind," Justin said.

"No, I want to go. I will choose."

TWENTY-EIGHT

"Lilliana, I want your opinion on a purchase I recently made." Marie dragged her granddaughter down the hall to the salon where the Madeline statue stood. "You must be honest about your feelings."

Marie whipped open the door with overwhelming flare. Slowly, Lilliana advanced into the room. After circling the statue once, she looked to her grandmother.

"What do you think?"

"It's recently done."

"Lilliana, I'm not asking you to date it. The artist is current-day and he's not immortal like us. *Non, non.* I want to know what you think of the subject."

"Is this one of Father's old lovers?"

"How did you know that?"

"Because you take perverse pleasure in irking Father whenever you can."

"Lilliana, this has nothing to do with pissing off Louis. Not anymore, anyway. I want you to tell me what you think of the subject." Marie walked over to her granddaughter and pushed her to take one more walk around the statue.

"There's a trick to this," Lilliana said while circling the statue.

"Just tell me what you think of the subject. Is she pretty? Is she beautiful? I guess I can't expect you to say she's not either."

"You're in competition with this woman?"

"For what? An idiot sculpturer who doesn't have a true eye for beauty?"

"Grandmother, who is this artist that you've taken up with?"

"He took me. Charged an outrageous amount for this statue."

Lilliana sighed.

"Come on, tell me what you think of her."

"She has beautiful features but is a bit plump."

"Plump! Where? She has a woman's figure, not that of a child. Which, by the way, is what she really has. Skinny. Lots of bones protruding here and there."

"Grandmother, have you seen this woman in person?"

"Yes, but I'll admit not naked. But even with clothes on, you can see how scrawny she is."

"If he's a good sculptor, the statue should be accurate."

"She wouldn't pose for him. He did her face from memory, but the body was his own wet dream."

They heard the front door open but couldn't distinguish what was being said in the hall until the intruders were almost upon the salon.

"I, at least, am a good host and can offer a variety of drinks."

"What's down here?"

A boy appeared at the salon's threshold.

"Grandmother, is this someone you've invited into the house?" asked Lilliana.

"No, I have," said Sade, coming into view along with Justin.

Marie leaned against her granddaughter. "I may faint."

"Who are these people?"

"Madeline," said the tall, handsome man whose eyes glittered an unnaturally beautiful green.

"You lied to me, Sade. What is this?" He pointed at the statue.

"Not mine. Belongs to Marie, or would you rather call her mother?"

"Louis, you are making more than one enemy here," said Marie.

"Grandmother, is he your son?"

"He's the son of the woman who belongs to the body I'm currently using. He was kind enough to stake his mother for me. By the way, Justin, she still creeps up on me once in a while, trying to take her body back. I get horrendous headaches then. She's testy about having been staked, I think. Especially since I've also defeated her spirit."

Felix took a few steps closer to the statue.

"Have you seen a woman who looks like this at the brothel, Felix?" Justin asked.

"Brothel! What would a child like this be doing in a brothel?" Lilliana asked.

"Servicing clients, probably," Marie said. "Don't look offended, Lilliana. He's old enough to pleasure certain gentlemen." Her eyes focused on Sade.

"I found him at Justin's," Sade said. "Dressed in a robe."

Lilliana marched over to the man Sade had just pointed at.

"You are disgusting. Only a pig would consider using a child." She lifted her hand to slap his face but hesitated, realizing that the show of temper would not ease any of the boy's problems.

"I rescued Felix from the brothel, mademoiselle. I rescued him before Sade could pick up the boy. Evidently, Sade paid well for the boy."

Lilliana whirled around to face Sade.

"Father?"

"You do this to me every time, Marie."

"Grandmother has nothing to do with this, Father. I want to know whether you purchased this boy for your own use."

"The child was being kept at a brothel that Marie and I occasionally visit." Sade was briefly interrupted by a giant harrumph from Marie. "I heard about the boy and wondered what I could do to help. Of course, the owners of the brothel had to be paid something to set the boy free. How could I know that they still kept the child? I paid to have him sent home, and quite a bit extra for their trouble."

"And you wonder why I don't believe you, Sade, when you say you don't know where Madeline is," Justin said.

"None of us believes you, Louis." Marie walked over to the boy and settled a hand on his dark, curly mop of hair. "He is a pleasure to look at, though. Can't blame you, Louis, for having a bit of a crush."

"I've never seen the boy before today," Sade seethed.

"I'm totally confused," said Lilliana.

"Sade purchased the boy sight unseen. I knew Sade would come looking for his property, so I took the boy home with me."

"You expected to make more money off the boy?" Lilliana asked.

"No. I want Madeline back."

"Who is Madeline?"

Marie spun her granddaughter around to face the statue.

"The woman who inspired this work?"

Justin moved closer to Lilliana.

"She couldn't have posed for this statue, because—"

"She's too scrawny," interrupted Marie.

"At one time, Madeline had been one of Sade's lovers in Albi before the cathedral was destroyed," explained Justin. "We came here to Paris together because she was too embarrassed to return to her family."

"Now she has left you and you blame my father?"

"You must know what he is," Justin said.

"I'm a father who wouldn't think of abusing a

child," Sade said. "The two women who live with me can tell you that there is no Madeline living here besides this inanimate statue. You may apologize, Justin."

"He's right," Lilliana said, looking at Justin. Her heart softened when she saw the pain on the young man's face. "I'm sorry. This woman must mean a lot to you. Why would you think she'd come back to live with my father?"

"Silly question," Sade muttered, but Lilliana ignored him.

"She left in a hurry, and the deaths that are taking place in Paris made me think that they might have been committed by an untrained vampire," said Justin.

"Madeline sucking the life out of the city's population. Somehow that doesn't ring true to me," said Sade. "Besides, I would never desert someone I've changed. That's something Marie would do."

"Father, this man is very serious, and all you're doing is making jokes." Lilliana returned her attention to Justin. "Were you and Madeline in love?"

She saw the young man take a swallow. Answering would not be easy for him.

"We needed each other," he finally replied.

"I doubt that either of you was honest with the other. Did you two make love?"

"That's a very dumb and personal question, Lilliana," Sade said.

Justin shook his head.

"What a waste," Sade shouted.

"I couldn't put her life at risk," Justin whispered.

"Then you are in love." Lilliana turned toward Sade. "We must help him find her. If she has been turned, we can help her."

"He'd rather stake her," Sade said.

"Grandmother, where did you get the statue?"

Marie felt bewildered. How did she get rooked into saving the scrawny redhead?

"It's important that you tell us, Grandmother, because the sculptor may know where she is staying. Could she even be with him? Is he one of us?"

"No. She had been a student of his and he had a crush on her." Marie shrugged. "She didn't even pose for the statue. Ask Louis or even Justin. She's much skinnier than this."

"But we must talk to the sculptor. Where does he live?" Lillian asked.

"I know," Justin said.

TWENTY-NINE

"No, child, you don't just move around clumps of clay to be doing something."

"I'm frustrated, Jacques. Why don't we take a break?" The young woman flung her arms about his neck.

"We don't have time, *chère*. Your lesson is almost over."

"But I can stay late. No one will be expecting me home. I told them that I'd be stopping at the museum to do some study."

"That is an excellent idea. The best you've come up with." Jacques pulled her arms from around his neck. "Sometimes I must give you lessons, or your parents will be wasting their money."

"Ah, Jacques, I like the naughty lessons that you give." She snuggled her face into his shoulder.

Jacques checked the time. A prissy matron would be arriving for her lesson in fifteen minutes. He didn't want her to get the idea that there might be additional benefits to taking lessons with him.

"Not today, *chère*."

"You keep sending me away hungry, Jacques." She began peeling off her shirt.

"You are not my only student."

She dropped the shirt to the floor and stood brazenly in a lacy, white bra that contrasted perfectly with her salon bought tan. "You have someone coming that you prefer over me?"

Jacques sighed. "No, I have a student coming who pays as much for my time as your parents do. On with the shirt."

The student unzipped her jeans. She never wore underpants, and before Jacques had thought it convenient, but now he simply tugged her jeans higher up on her hips and tried to budge the zipper that refused to move.

"You've ruined my jeans, Jacques. I'll have to take them off while you find another pair for me to wear."

"*Mais non,* leave your shirt hanging out and no one will be able to see." He bent over to pick up her shirt, and she swept one of her legs between his, throwing him off balance. She giggled as they fell to the floor.

She managed to release his staff and slide down to greet it with open mouth. Jacques decided to give up.

Her head bobbed and the doorbell rang.

"*Merde,*" Jacques cursed. He pushed her away.

"If we are very quiet, she'll go away," she said.

"And I will be short money for the day."

He threw her shirt over her breasts and tidied himself.

At the door, he took another look back to make sure she had dressed. She buttoned the last button and stuck her tongue out at him. Relieved, Jacques threw open the door and stared into a mob, led by Justin.

"I told you I have no idea where Madeline is." He looked into each of the faces but paused when he met his client's eyes.

"Jacques, I told these people that you had no idea where Madeline is, but they refused to believe me." She turned back to the crowd to make an announcement. "Jacques has asked me to pose for him. And he said he would give me the final product without any cost to me, because he wants so much to mold my body with his hands." She belligerently looked back at Jacques.

"*Oui.* We just recently made the arrangement," Jacques said.

"He doesn't have time for Madeline anymore, nor for this snippet," Marie growled, seeing the young student who had joined them at the door.

"What's a snippet, Jacques? How many students were you expecting?" the girl asked.

"Friends, this is my studio and my home. At this time of day, it is a studio where I work and give lessons. I don't entertain during these hours, but please call for an appointment and somehow I'll manage to fit you all into my schedule—but not today."

Justin pushed his way into the studio, followed by the others.

"You never mentioned the statue to me," said Justin.

"You don't have enough money to pay for such a collectible as the Madeline statue. Why would I have offered it to you?" Jacques said.

"Madeline didn't pose for it, did she?" Justin asked.

"Oh, my Lord. Madeline has been with Louis. How could you worry about her posing for a statue?" said Marie. "Jacques would never be capable of coming up with the lascivious acrobatics Louis could dream up."

Jacques knew that what he'd just received was no compliment, yet he did think the remark might save his life.

"Grandmother, that's cruel."

"Was it?" Jacques's client looked around with round eyes. "I'm sure Louis doesn't think so."

"Justin, I would love to reunite you with Madeline and gain some peace and quiet, but I can't do it." Jacques knew that he'd never see Madeline again if the two were to rejoin.

THIRTY

Miriam shuffled along as quickly as the heavy bag over her right shoulder allowed. She prided herself on being on time for appointments, but today she'd be late. Miriam wouldn't have been late but for the fat, old man living above her. He had lost his wife several months before and now relied on most of the women in the building to shop, cook, and even clean for him. Initially, the women felt sorry for him. One or two even considered moving in with him until they had spent more than a couple of hours with his grumpiness. He took advantage, and that had to stop.

Calling her upstairs to his apartment to help with the laundry took things too far. She'd set him straight tonight when she brought up his dinner, she thought. *Dinner. He makes me late for my sculpting class and I think about cooking him dinner.* She had to be mad. Jacques might allow her to stay an extra few minutes, but she'd be more than twenty minutes late, and he certainly would have another student to teach.

Miriam almost stepped out in front of a car, except the driver rapidly hit his horn.

Go, go, she wanted to scream. She checked her watch. Yes, she'd be at least twenty minutes late, with no real excuse except for a lazy septuagenarian.

Before crossing the street, she checked for traffic. When assured that she could safely make it to the other side, she crossed.

In her mind she inventoried everything she had put in her bag, making sure she had left nothing behind.

"Oooops," she muttered to herself, seeing a dark head bob from between two parked cars. She wondered if the young man lay in wait for a passerby. Today so many foreigners entered the country, and none of them could be trusted.

Stepping out into the street, Miriam began to cross to the opposite side. The young man between the cars didn't bother to follow her.

What a relief, she thought, glad that she didn't have to dig down inside her coat for her police whistle.

In her mind she recapped what she planned on doing at Jacques's studio. She wished she could carry her piece home, but she might be tempted to work without Jacques's instructions and ruin what she had spent the last few months working on.

She saw the vacant lot and knew she had only three more blocks to go. This area of Paris always looked dreary, not necessarily unsafe but haunted. *Yes, haunted.* Most of the residents kept their shutters closed even on fine sunny days, and children never played in the street. She couldn't even be sure children lived here.

A dog howled on the first floor of the building she passed, making her cringe and pull her coat tighter around herself. The dog continued to bay, and she picked up her pace.

A tuxedo cat ran across her path with such lightening speed that she paused for a second.

Thank goodness the cat had some white on its breast and paws, she thought.

An object rolled passed her as if it had been kicked, but she heard nothing else. No steps, no talking, no . . . *Wait,* she thought. Barely audible, the sound grew closer. She wished that she hadn't worn heels. Not only weren't they comfortable, but if she needed to run they would slow her down. Remembering the man between the two parked cars, she considered kicking her shoes off, dropping the bag, and making an all-out run. If anyone watched, they would think she was crazy. On the other hand, her life meant more to her than what people thought.

Miriam dropped the bag onto the sidewalk and kicked off her pumps. She took one broad step before being tackled to the ground. Her hands went immediately to her skirt, hoping to prevent rape. The person above her chuckled. A silly kid trying to scare her?

He began tearing at her throat, his long nails slashing at her flesh. She attempted to scream, but he twisted her face into the cement beneath them. He pawed with one hand at her throat like an animal, until finally she felt blood rolling across the front of her neck. He settled his body heavily upon hers and nuzzled his face into her neck, lapping, sucking, licking. She heard him gurgle from all the blood he took into his mouth, but no breath touched her flesh. The thing didn't breathe. She fought to free her arms, but when she finally got one from beneath her body she found nothing to grasp. She couldn't reach his hair that fell onto her cheeks and forehead.

Tired. Unusually tired. She had barely enough strength now to catch her own breath.

THIRTY-ONE

Yvette's father waited.

"Let me take you to school, Yvette," he had said. "Let me pick you up also, until the police get the person who killed your mother and brother."

She had violently shaken her head no. She complained of looking infantile in front of her friends.

Infantile, he thought. She would always be his infant, even on her forty-third birthday, if God permitted him to live that long.

He hadn't returned to work yet and didn't have the energy to clean the house. He could only wait.

He walked to the window to check for schoolchildren. Only the vendors and shoppers cluttered the streets with their food carts and packages. Several cars had difficulty making it down the street, because the shoppers paid no mind to traffic when heading for a sale. Now and then a stray cat or dog would try to swipe some food while no one watched.

The father walked back to his chair and pressed his fingers into the back of it, squeezing as hard as he could. The tension would make him ill if he didn't use self-control.

He checked the clock. Another sixteen minutes and she'd be bouncing into the apartment looking for something to eat. He'd take her out tonight for a special meal. He'd even let her choose the restaurant. He let go of the chair and walked around front to plop into the seat. Closing his eyes, he thought of the past and allowed visions of his wife and son to run rampant through his thoughts.

Time escaped him until he heard the children from the above apartment come home. They were older than Yvette and got home later. He opened his eyes and checked the clock. Yvette should have been home twenty minutes ago.

No, don't be a fool. Children often linger, not thinking about a waiting parent. But she knows the danger out on the street and should have come directly home. He'd chastise her. *She has to learn to come directly home for her own safety.*

His legs felt like jelly. He wanted to stand but couldn't.

He had never spanked her before, but . . .

"But, monsieur, your daughter has been missing for only a few hours. She may be with a friend. Have you called some of the other parents? She could be at the home of a school friend and not be paying attention to time." The gendarme tried to calm the father, fetching coffee, resting a hand on the father's shoulder, and offering alternatives for where the child might be.

"*Non.* Possibly she might linger a few minutes at school, but she would never be more than an hour late. The child knows how I worry."

"Children sometimes don't understand our worries as parents. My son often arrives for dinner late, and what can we do? We scold, but also wait to have our dinner."

"No. I've lost my wife and son, my daughter's mother and brother. She understands."

"Is there someone, monsieur, who would purposefully kidnap the child?"

"What do you mean?"

"Have you made enemies?"

"Not the kind who would kill or kidnap my family."

"If you were so worried, why did you permit her to travel back and forth to school alone?"

"She refused my company. I thought she'd be traveling crowded streets, and often she meets with classmates on the way to school."

"Have you spoken to any of the other parents as I suggested?"

"Of course. No one has seen her since this morning. I contacted the school, and they told me that she'd attended all her classes. They didn't notice anything unusual about her."

"And relatives?"

"Except for an aunt, I've spoken to everyone."

"Ah, the aunt perhaps . . ."

"She works long hours and is always hard to reach. But there would be no reason for her to pick Yvette up. The aunt and I have come to an understanding."

"Which is?"

The father hesitated, staring off at a wall covered with notices, the papers layered so much that he wondered how the pushpins managed to hold the bulky weights up.

"She wanted to care for Yvette for a while."

"Lessen the burden on you, monsieur?"

"She doesn't trust me. I don't know why. But I made it clear to her that Yvette would stay with me."

"May I suggest you pay this aunt a visit?"

"You think she may have taken Yvette? But that would be too cruel. She knows how much Yvette and I love each other, and Yvette would clamor to come home."

"I am only suggesting that you seek this aunt's help, since she also appears to have great love for Yvette."

"I don't want her help. I want yours."

"If the girl is not home by the morning, come in again."

"She'll be dead by then."

"Monsieur?"

"She's a good child, not any sort of delinquent. She must be in trouble if she hasn't come home."

"I have filled in all the necessary paperwork, and we will begin the search in the morning if you do not find her before then."

The father stood and made a move toward the gendarme.

"It will be better if you are waiting at home for Yvette than in one of our cells."

THIRTY-TWO

"You know something, Marie."

"Louis?"

Sade threw one of his legs over the arm of the leather chair and steepled his fingers.

"You have the statue of Madeline. You have an interesting acquaintanceship with the sculptor. He is even willing to spend tedious time with you to salve your ego. Why, Marie?"

"Jacques and I met at one of the gallery parties. He mentioned the statue of Madeline and couldn't stop talking about it. I became curious and wanted to see it. I didn't even have any intention of purchasing anything, but I longed for the statue as soon as I laid eyes on it. Didn't you feel the same way when you first saw the living, breathing Madeline?"

Sade ignored the question as one of Marie's gibes.

"And why would Jacques do a statue of you, Marie?

You never mentioned anything about posing until we got to Jacques's studio."

"I wanted to surprise you. I thought of putting it into your room, right up close to your coffin. You'd swing open the lid, and I'd be the first sight you'd see." She smiled.

"Please don't cause me to be ill." Sade reached over and took a deep drink from his water glass. He gave a slight cough before returning the glass to the table. "And why would Jacques be willing to sculpt you for free?"

Marie rose from the sofa on which she had been seated, did a slow twirl, and looked back at Sade.

"You haven't answered my question, Marie."

"Don't be coy, Louis, the answer is in front of you."

"We're helping him," Lilliana announced from the doorway before seating herself on the sofa. "Justin needs our help. We should be brainstorming, remembering rumors or recalling old friends . . ." She stopped and looked squarely at Sade. She pulled her grandmother down onto the sofa next to her. "Who might be responsible for the killings?"

Marie rested her hand on her granddaughter's arm.

"Sweetest, we are vampires. We keep a low profile. We don't piss off our peers." She watched her granddaughter give a side glance in the direction of Sade. "Most of our peers. If Louis and I began asking questions, we'd be suspect."

"That's a silly excuse, Grandmother. Most of the

139

vampires in Paris fear you and Father. You dislike Justin and don't want to help him."

"True."

"Father is a far more forgiving person than you, Grandmother, because he is going to help."

"Have you volunteered, Louis?" Marie asked.

Lilliana crossed her arms in front of her and waited.

"Lilliana, your grandmother is rarely right, but this time she may be."

Lilliana stood. "I will help Justin."

"But, child, you have recently arrived back in Paris. Most of the vampires don't even recognize you," pleaded Sade.

Lilliana crossed the room and fell to her knees in front of Sade.

"Father, do you remember what it was like when we thought we'd be separated forever?"

Marie moaned.

"Please, let's not bore your grandmother with what it feels like to love someone. I'll help, but only because it's important to you."

"And who knows, you may get another shot at Madeline." Marie glared at Sade. "Besides, I have loved many people, Louis. You and Lilliana, for instance."

Lilliana stood and ran to hug her grandmother.

"Thank you so much for helping, Grandmother. Justin couldn't have done anything so terrible to you that you'd condemn him to be without his love."

"Yes, he has."

"Grandmother, I would think he would have greater

reason to be angry with you. You stole his mother's body."

"It was the only one I could find that was not in use at the time. What could you expect? I couldn't bear being between worlds."

"Someday we all will be."

"I hate when you're depressed, Louis. You always want to spread the infection."

THIRTY-THREE

Madeline watched as he slipped into the house. Blood soaked his clothes and hair. At that moment she couldn't go to him. She couldn't accept what he had just done. She sat down on the top step of the staircase and waited to see what he would do.

Like an animal's, his tongue flicked out to lick his exposed skin. He swayed in the center of the hall, hair falling into his face, his long, brittle nails scraping across his cheeks.

Bile filled her mouth as she fought for control, looking away from him in hopes of erasing the vision.

Soft whimpers forced her to look back at the scene. Sensing her presence, he threw back his hair and looked up at her. The pale stain of blood darkened his features. His eyes pleaded for help, but still she would not stand to take him into her arms.

"Madeline," he said.

She used her hands to cover her mouth to prevent the sobs that closed up her throat.

"Madeline," he repeated. "I can't stop. There's never enough blood. The woman tonight—"

"Shut up!" She rose to her feet. "I don't want you to speak of her or of any of the . . ."

"Victims," he said softly, lowering his head like a chastised child. "I don't want to drink their blood. I try to sit upstairs in the room and wait for you. I pace the room, the hall, the staircase, counting the minutes, knowing that you haven't deserted me. I love you for that, Madeline."

"If you love me, why don't you obey?"

He raised his head and peered into the darkness in which she stood. His eyes gleamed with confidence. "Because I'm sure you will stay with me."

She began to walk down the stairs, never looking away from his eyes.

"Then you aren't trying hard enough."

"You've watched me kill, Madeline. Yes, you've reached out to drag me back away from the poor victims. Yet there is nothing you can do. You aren't strong enough to overpower me. Memories stop you from destroying me, even though our past days together can never be the same again. I'll not ask to be freed. I'm afraid of death."

"Do you want to live this way?"

"If I must. Could you destroy me?"

They stood inches apart. She recognized his shaded

143

features and the tone of his voice. She had been an in-
quisitive child on tiptoe peeking into his crib. The blue
blanket had shivered with his jerky movements. His
face had seemed so far away then. She had wanted to
touch him to make sure he was real.

She raised her hand, hesitated. Hesitated too long,
for she dropped her hand back by her side.

"Are you Matthew?" she asked.

"I'm his personal demon."

THIRTY-FOUR

The father pounded on his sister-in-law's apartment door. He heard the chimes within the apartment count out midnight.

"Damn, Babbette, you must be in there. Open the door."

A man who lived at the opposite end of the hall came out of his apartment dressed in only pajama bottoms. A red and black demon glared from his broad, hairy chest. The tattoo rippled with the flexing of his muscles.

"My daughter is missing, monsieur. I think Babbette could help me find her."

"More likely that's the gendarmes' job," the man said.

"Babbette is the girl's aunt, my sister-in-law. She would want to know if something has happened to Yvette."

"I'm sure she would have opened the door to you by now if she were home."

How could the father explain the complications that prevented Babbette from responding to him?

"Speak to the gendarmes, monsieur. If you persist in keeping me awake, I will call them for you."

Do that, then! almost passed the father's lips. *Let them catch Babbette keeping my daughter from me.* What was he doing? If Yvette were in Babbette's apartment, she would have heard the ruckus. There's no way Babbette could have prevented his daughter from coming to the door.

"I'm sorry I woke you." The father turned to the elevator. A light tap of his finger on the call button and the doors immediately opened. He walked onto the elevator. The doors closed, and he stood patiently, forgetting to press the ground-floor button.

He'd returned home several times hoping to find Yvette waiting for him, but the apartment remained empty. Doors gaped open to closets glutted with his wife's and son's clothes. He'd barely touch an outfit before tears blinded him. He might have to move out and leave the clothes behind.

The elevator began to descend, stopping finally at the first floor. When the doors opened, he faced two gendarmes.

"I'm leaving. My daughter is not here."

"Excuse me, monsieur, you are coming from which apartment?"

The father told the gendarmes.

"We should all go back, monsieur." The gendarmes placed their hands on his shoulders and backed him into the elevator.

THIRTY-FIVE

"Have you found your Madeline, Justin?" Gerard alighted from the darkness of the night.

"Are you out on the hunt?"

"I found my quarry." Gerard looped his arm with Justin's. He guided Justin down to the Seine. "There have been more killings. The animal is becoming more brutal with each kill."

"I've not been reading the papers."

"Nor searching the streets for the guilty party. Madeline takes up too much of your time. Finding her will not save lives. She may be a young woman who wants to live her life without the chains of love. So many women do these days. In my youth, a woman would be considered a slut if she lived on her own and taunted men with her freedom."

"And when were you young?"

"Centuries ago." Gerard smiled. "Has Sade not come for the boy?"

"He doesn't have Madeline."

"Are you sure?"

Justin pulled away.

"You may have Madeline, for all I know."

"I wish I did. I would return her to you in order to have you back on the streets searching for the person killing all these mortals."

"Not that you care about their lives."

"No. I am honest. I care whether my own kind are finally outed."

"And mostly for your own sake, I would guess."

"I have a bond with my fellow blood drinkers, Justin. The thirst is real for me and for them. Real enough that we temper our appetites. You've tasted blood, Justin. You're familiar with the hunger, perhaps not to the extent of a true vampire but enough to realize we wouldn't waste a precious drop. This fiend splatters blood around like a child playing in the mud."

"He or she may be a renegade vampire. Think of Marissa."

"No, those are always destroyed by their own kind."

"So much for the bonding."

"Don't chide me, Justin. I have assisted you in finding Sade because you were sure he would either have Madeline or know where she was. Now it seems you were wrong, true?"

"I'll never believe Sade."

"What will you do? Follow him? Wait on street corners while he takes his hedonistic pleasure at clubs and brothels? Accept that he may have bested you. I have done so on many occasions."

"You're a loser. I am not."

Gerard backhanded Justin. Justin stayed on his feet but felt the blood dripping down from his nose.

"If we ever end up in a contest, Justin, you will lose."

"Here's some of your precious blood, Gerard. Luxuriate in its taste by licking my fingers."

"Yes, test me, Justin, while I still need you."

"Why can't you find this murderer?"

"You are expert at catching us in the act. I expect you also to be able to find this fiend. Also, if it is a vampire causing these deaths, I may not be able to kill him or her."

"Why not?"

"I never injure my own children."

"You killed Marissa."

"She was not mine. She was one of Marie's insults."

"Sade's mother-in-law?"

Gerard nodded. "She, too, is back in Paris."

"Do you expect me to cringe in fear?"

"How well do you know Sade and Marie?"

"It is not important that you have that knowledge, Justin. We agreed about what your job was, and you haven't found the killer yet."

"I'll find Madeline first."

"And let many more die? She's a woman, Justin, not the only woman. As much as you love her, you may not be able to have her."

Justin felt his body tremble with the sound of Gerard's words.

"I must get home to the boy."

"The chattel the brothel was keeping for Sade?"

Justin nodded.

"Sade did not take the boy from you?" Wonder lit up Gerard's eyes. He broke out in laughter. "Maybe I underestimate you, Justin."

THIRTY-SIX

The gendarmes unlocked Babbette's apartment door and invited the father to enter. He assumed that one of the tenants in the building had called the gendarmes.

"My name is Jean Chartres. Babbette is my sister-in-law. I came here looking for my daughter, who is missing. I didn't mean to disturb anyone else in the building, but I felt so frustrated. . . ."

"Please sit down, Monsieur Chartres, while we look around."

"But I haven't taken anything. I don't have a key, and it's obvious the apartment hasn't been broken into."

"Is it, monsieur?"

"You had to use the key. The door hadn't been left ajar." Jean paused to think. "Why do you have the key? Did the building manager give it to you?"

The gendarmes didn't answer. One walked from

room to room, and the other stayed with Jean in the living room.

Jean saw nothing out of the ordinary. Babbette's meticulous neatness always made Jean uncomfortable. He yearned to prop his feet up on the polished coffee table, perhaps move the floral centerpiece to the side to make room for his work shoes. The polished wood floors and expensive rugs always looked freshly cleaned.

"There is no one here," said the gendarme who had made the search.

"Monsieur Chartres, why would you believe that you would find your daughter here?"

"Because I had nowhere else to look. I'd been to see the gendarmes, and they weren't helpful, so I continued my search on my own. Besides, I haven't been able to reach Babbette all day."

"And her husband?"

"Reginald? I never speak to him. He tends to board himself up in the den when company comes over. He makes a brief appearance at the dinner table and then excuses himself."

"Did Reginald and Babbette get along?"

"Yes, I think she liked all his eccentricities. The weirder people are, the more she likes them. He also came with lots of money."

"Do you know where we could find Reginald?"

"He should be home. Both of them should be home by now." The father's body stiffened. "Has something happened to them? How did you get the key? Please, I must know what is happening. My daughter is also missing."

"Also, monsieur?"

"Obviously, Babbette and Reginald aren't here, and I'm beginning to think that you weren't called by any of the neighbors."

"Why would the neighbors call us?"

"Damn, can't you do anything but answer my questions with your own?"

"You seem to think that the neighbors would have called us had they seen you."

"I made a ruckus earlier banging on Babbette's door. I thought she might be here and refusing to answer. The neighbor down the hall came out of his apartment to remind me how late it was. That's when I came to my senses and decided to check back home for my daughter. Instead, I ran into both of you downstairs."

"You are married to Babbette's sister?"

"I'm widowed."

"For how long?"

"Recently. My wife and son were killed by the maniac that's been terrorizing Paris. That's why I'm worried about my daughter. I thought Babbette may have taken her."

"Come with us, Monsieur Chartres. We will need you to make a statement."

THIRTY-SEVEN

Justin reached into his pocket for the key to the garret. He heard loud music and smelled freshly popped popcorn. He closed his eyes and hoped Felix hadn't already made the transition to typical teenager.

Instead, he found Felix scrubbing down the floors.

"What are you doing?" Justin asked.

"I'm proving how handy I can be. I like living here. You don't require anything of me. I'm not sure about that Monsieur Sade. I don't trust him. He's lied to you, hasn't he? He may try to talk you into giving me to him."

Justin gently closed the door behind him.

"Felix, you needn't turn yourself into my slave or personal servant. I will not give you to Sade."

"But what if he does have Madeline? He may offer to trade."

"I doubt he knows where Madeline is." Justin found

155

himself tiptoeing across the freshly washed floor. "And you I should bring into the child authorities. They'll find you a better home than I can give you."

"No, Monsieur Justin. They may send me back to my uncles, who will either sell me back into slavery or harm me in a worse way. They have killed before. I heard my parents speak of the crimes my uncles committed. Even they feared my uncles."

"Do you think your uncles had anything to do with your parents' deaths?"

The boy became quiet, dropping the washrag he had been using into the bucket of soapy water. He leaned back to rest on his haunches before answering.

"I only know that my parents died in an automobile accident." His sad eyes briefly caught Justin's gaze before he looked back down at the wood floor.

"You do think they had something to do with the deaths, don't you?"

Fear tightened the boy's features as he peered up at Justin.

"My parents told me nothing. I would only overhear a few words they spoke to each other late at night when they thought I slept."

"Mind if I turn down the radio?"

The boy jumped to his feet, ran to the radio, and turned it off.

"I'm sorry. The music helps me to keep moving while I'm cleaning. I imagine I am somewhere else, not down on my knees polishing a floor."

"Play the music, Felix. But you might want to lower

the sound a bit next time. Neither of us want neighbors knocking on the door."

The boy shook his head so violently that his curls bobbed around his head, settling into a twisted mass of confusion.

"We do have a problem here, though. What should I do with you?"

"I can learn to cook," the boy enthusiastically offered.

Justin laughed.

"But who will teach you?"

"What about the lady who is Sade's daughter? She likes us. She offered to help you find Madeline. Why wouldn't she teach me to cook?"

"We don't even know whether she can cook."

"All women know how to cook. My father said it was in their genes. Men have more important things to do."

"What did your mother say about that?"

"She would shake her head and go back to the kitchen."

"Leave the floor, Felix, and come sit on the bed." Justin plopped himself into the chair.

The boy looked at his hands and his dirty clothes.

"I'm not clean enough to sit on the bed. Mom would kill me if she saw me do that." Instead, he sat on the floor facing Justin.

"I guess we'll both be learning from each other," Justin said.

"Didn't your mother hate it when your clothes were dirty?" the boy asked.

"My mother didn't worry about being a good house-wife or mother."

"Is she still alive?"

"It's complicated, Felix."

The boy tilted his head.

"Either you're alive or dead, right? Unless she's in a coma."

"Yes, Felix, a coma. She's not able to speak to me anymore. I don't even know whether she is aware of me at all."

"But at least you have the chance that she might get better because she's not dead."

"Her coma, as we shall call it, is my fault. I shouldn't have been weak. I could have given her peace, and instead I've locked her into a more frightening world than the one she already had."

"Do you talk to her?"

"Talk to her?"

"I've read that when a person is in a coma, family members should tell stories to the person and remind the comatose of things that happened in the past. Maybe she will hear you and want to come back."

"Marie will make sure that will never happen."

"How can she?"

"Because my mother is in Marie's care."

"Your mother lives in the same house as Sade?"

"Yes."

The boy thought a long time about this.

"Then give me to Sade."

"What?"

"If I live with them, I can help you to reach your mother. If they think I like being with them, they'll give me the run of the house, and I can tell you where they keep your mother. I can talk to her for you and prepare the way."

Justin rumpled the boy's hair.

"There are many secrets I cannot share with you. But always remember that no one at Sade's house can be trusted, and don't ever talk about sacrificing yourself like that. They are inhumane and without morals. They enjoy watching others suffer. You are too young to trade your life for a woman who will never find salvation."

"What has your mother done that is so wrong?"

"She is very much like Sade and his family."

"Did she make you suffer?"

"In many ways. I still suffer for her. She's a ghost in my life. Always with me. Always blaming me for what has happened to her."

"What did you do to her?"

Justin leaned back in his chair and sighed.

"If I admitted to you what I have done, you would probably leave me to live with Sade."

"No, I wouldn't. Sade doesn't feel sorry for anything he has done. You do."

"Being contrite doesn't change the past, Felix."

"But it might prevent you from repeating the past."

THIRTY-EIGHT

Madeline watched him sleep. She placed her hand on his chest but found no movement. He didn't breathe; he never flinched while he slept. He appeared to be a waxwork of a human. He lay on a thin layer of soil that they had spread over the sheets. French soil. Moist now since they had freshly replaced the old soil. His hands held clots of the soil that spilled between his fingers. The soil stuck to his jeans and marred the whiteness of his shirt.

Often she would sit by his bed until he fell into the death trance. She hated being in the room with him when he slept. She hated being a sentinel for the dead.

She stood to leave but couldn't. She walked over to the bed and brushed his long hair back from his face. The pallid complexion and placid features didn't belong to him. They were a mask that hid his true self from her. Blood stained his lower lip, looking like stale

160

blotted lipstick. Pale flecks of hair covered his cheeks and chin. He'd never grow a true beard, only an adolescent version of a man's beard.

She held his hands in hers. His long nails, discolored with a mixture of soil and blood, reminded her of his hunger. He used the solid nails to slit open the skin of his victims. He tore at bodies with his teeth and nails. She squeezed his hands hard, but he did not wake. He trusted her to watch over him.

Madeline had watched him kill more than once but had never been able to stop him. When he hungered, he had a superhuman power. He barely recognized her, and had on several occasions struck out at her. Jacques had recently commented about a bruise on her leg. She lied and said that she had fallen. Once Matthew had smacked her so hard that she thought her cheekbone might have been broken, but after the swelling went down and the bruise healed, her face appeared normal. He didn't mean to harm her, but his hands were not his own when the hunger took him. She raised his hands to her lips and kissed them. They matched her hands in size but would have been so much larger if he had been allowed to live out his life. Once these hands had been baby-sized, and she had held them as he learned to walk. Not being much older than he, her efforts sometimes seemed wasted. Were her efforts now wasted and misguided? Should she bring Justin here? Justin would know how to end the agony.

Carefully, she laid his hands back on his abdomen.

If she went to Justin, she wouldn't have to continue with the embarrassment of posing for Jacques. She wouldn't have to assist in the murder of innocents. She'd be able to return to the garret and sleep beside Justin. And what? Be relieved that this boy's soul finally lay at rest. Existed no more in this world.

Softly, she ran the tips of her fingers across his cold cheeks, the skin like marble in the intensity of its coldness. Once his skin burned beneath her palm when a terrible fever had overtaken his healthy body. His ruddy complexion had become flushed with the disease that almost took his life. Now, God forgive her, she wished he had died. At least then he would have died in the grace of God. Now only hell awaited him. And her, she reminded herself.

Should she have talked to Justin before leaving? Should she have trusted Justin's counsel? But what if he had given her only one choice? Would she have abided with what he suggested, or would she still have run away?

She looked down at the vampire before her and couldn't imagine staking his poor, young heart. Justin would have advised her to let go. There is nothing to be gained from keeping this vampire alive. She only robbed Satan of this soul for a time. Eventually, the devil would win out.

Her tears fell on his cheeks. How she wished they could perform miracles and save his soul. Seated on the bed, she bent over to kiss both his cheeks.

He had Mom's nose and Dad's big ears, but they

shared the same long lashes and green eyes. Only, his hair was auburn and hers a natural carrot red.

Anyone looking at them, though, would recognize them as brother and sister.

Thirty-nine

Jacques paced his living room. Madeline had been due more than an hour ago. Had the foolish girl decided that she didn't need his money anymore? Perhaps she made more walking the streets of Paris, he speculated. If she didn't show soon, he'd give up on her and visit the café across the street, where he'd find solace with the new waitress who had been impressed with his paint-stained hands and jeans.

The doorbell rang, and he moved quickly down the hall to the front door. Pulling the door open, he started to berate the visitor, but stopped when he saw Marie.

"Testy today," she said, walking past him, peeling off her cashmere coat, and letting it drop to the marble floor.

"What are you doing here?" he asked.

"I've decided that we should start working on my statue. You know, the one you promised to do in return for my silence."

Jacques followed her to the living room.

"I can't do it today."

"Why not?" She abruptly turned to face him.

"My time is valuable, madame. Right now I should be working on a piece already in progress."

"Why aren't you?"

"The model didn't show," he said, walking over to the liquor cabinet.

"Sherry would be nice," she said. "There's a bit of a chill out there today."

"Madame's hands always seem cold." Jacques poured a whiskey for himself and a sherry for her.

"Yes, the rest of me feels just as cold. You should appreciate that, since you work in marble." She took the glass of sherry and raised it in a salute to Jacques, but he had already downed his double. "It's caused by a certain illness that is prevalent in the family. Several of us suffer from it."

"Madame, I am too upset to work today. We can plan to start on a day that is mutually convenient for the both of us."

"Madeline didn't show, did she?"

Jacques went back to the cabinet to pour himself another drink.

"The young woman wastes herself on inferior men," said Jacques.

"Inferior to whom? You?" Marie stood next to him, rubbing her hand across his ass. "Maybe you should increase the age of your liaisons, Jacques. Young women allow romance to blind them to the true expert lovers. You don't need anything from her. Except for sex, and she knows that. No, she wants the man who needs her support, her courage, even her money. She is the only one in the world who can save the loser, and he reinforces this concept daily."

"Is this coming from experience, madame?" Jacques swigged back another whiskey.

"I would never admit that, Jacques. I'd be a fool to admit to having been a fool."

"It would only acknowledge that you are human, madame."

"Jacques, I am not human." She slipped her hand between his thighs.

"I could spare perhaps . . ." Jacques checked the clock on the wall. "An hour."

"I don't expect you to be watching the clock, Jacques."

The doorbell rang. Marie dropped her hand to her side and waited.

"Call me a frustrated old man, madame, but I can't ignore the doorbell."

"Yes, you could." Her harsh voice made Jacques cringe slightly.

He decided not to give her the upper hand and went to open the door.

"I'm sorry, Jacques. We still have at least another forty-five minutes to work."

Madeline appeared to be out of breath. He noticed that she had been losing weight, her face slimmer, her body lankier.

"I should send you away without a cent. See what

your man would think of you if you came home with empty pockets."

By the time Madeline and Jacques entered the living room, Marie had poured herself another sherry.

"Madeline, this is a client. Madame de Montreuil. She has taken great interest in my work." He watched Marie turn to Madeline with an obviously forced smile.

"I know you," Madeline said. "I've seen you somewhere before."

"I am all over Paris, darling. I can't stay home." She turned back to pour another sherry. "Would you like a drink . . . I'm sorry, your name?"

"Madeline," Jacques muttered.

"Could you repeat that a little louder and clearer for me, Jacques?" Marie asked.

"I'm sure madame heard me the first time. And no, Madeline would not like a sherry. She and I have work to do. We have very little time left for today's session."

"Would you mind . . . Madeline, I believe is what you said, Jacques?" Marie looked at him, but he refused to respond. "Madeline, would you mind if I sat in on today's modeling? I've always wanted to watch a creative genius at work. Besides, he has promised to sculpt me one day when he can find the time."

"I'm sorry, madame. I hope I didn't interrupt a business discussion," Madeline said. "I can come back another day. It would be better for me if I could go home early."

"You come late and want to leave early. I would like to complete this work during my lifetime. How can I

capture your beauty and mood if I rarely see you?"
Jacques found himself waving his hands chaotically in
midair. When he saw how calm the two women
looked, he knew he had made a fool of himself.

"I only meant that you and Madame de Montreuil
should finish discussing whatever business you had
together."

Marie walked to the table where she had left her
purse. She undid the flap and searched inside.

"Tell me, Madeline, how much does Jacques usually
pay you?"

"Oh, I couldn't take any money today. I didn't do
anything."

"You made every effort to get here. When you first
entered the room, I could tell you were out of breath.
Isn't that right, Jacques? You should be paid. I imagine
Jacques doesn't pay you well as it is. Will this cover
what you would have made today?" Marie passed
money to Madeline, who at first hesitated but finally
took the money and thanked Marie.

"This is far more than Jacques pays. You must take
some back."

"No, Madeline. You are worth far more than what
Jacques pays you. Go home to your—"

"Gigolo," Jacques interrupted.

"Lover," Marie corrected. "Buy some wine. It is too
late for fresh fish, but butchers still will have some perfect cuts of beef."

"He probably doesn't need to be fattened up,"
Jacques growled.

"No, but Madeline could use a few pounds. Does Jacques run you ragged, darling?"

"She sits on a bench the whole time she is here, madame."

"But my guess is that she doesn't live anywhere near here. Do you, Madeline?"

"Not too far, madame."

"Which arrondissement?" Marie asked.

Madeline immediately thanked Marie for the money and promised Jacques that she would be on time the next day. Hurriedly, she made her way out of the room, down the hall, and out of the apartment.

"I tried, Jacques."

"You mean to get her address."

"Oui."

"Why should it matter to you, madame?"

"Curiosity. I wonder what kind of man would force a young woman such as her to leave Justin and pose for you."

"I don't like being lumped in the same sentence as Justin, madame."

Marie giggled, and Jacques could tell that she nearly burst into laughter.

"Never mind, Jacques. We now have the rest of the evening to start on my statue."

"No, madame. I have a new student coming. One of my long-term students fell victim to the serial killer terrorizing Paris. I needed to replace her."

"Oui, I read about the woman. Frightening to think it happened a short distance from here."

"I can walk you down to your car if you'd like."

"*Mai non,* I'm safe."

"Don't be so confident, madame. This murderer is supposed to be strong. He has also killed hefty men who should have been able to defend themselves. Allow me to walk you down."

"I'm not sure whether you want to make sure I go away or you're really worried about my safety."

"Both, madame. There's a bit of the gentleman still hidden inside me."

"Deep inside, I'd say." Marie picked up her purse. "Could you retrieve my coat?"

"It's where you left it, madame. We may pick it up on the way out."

"See what I mean? The gentleman in you has almost vanished. Your mother would be disappointed."

"I am often disappointed in my mother, madame. Her scowls and nagging drove me away into the arms of an older woman many years ago. I think of her fondly."

"Your mother?"

"The older woman, madame. My mother is still in my life, but the older woman . . ." He shrugged. "She may be six feet under by now."

Marie leaned her body against Jacques.

"Someday she may rise from the grave just to rekindle your old love affair."

"You warm my heart, madame, with your romanticism."

170

FORTY

"Monsieur Jean Chartres, this is not good that we should meet so often under such dreadful circumstances. First your wife and son are killed by this maniac we have roaming the Paris streets. And now just a few hours ago we find your sister-in-law dead, presumably killed by the same person. If we can even call this vicious animal a person. Ah, *oui,* your daughter is also missing."

"I came here earlier seeking help, and no one would listen."

"Monsieur Chartres, I am listening now."

"But it may be too late. You tell me that Babbette was seen picking up Yvette at school. What if the killer has Yvette?"

"Did you ask your sister-in-law to pick up your daughter, monsieur?"

"*Mais non.* I told you Yvette did not want someone

171

coming to the school for her or else I would have been there."

"Sometimes it is better, monsieur, not to allow children to have their way. But I am sorry. I didn't mean for it to sound accusatory. Please accept my apology?"

"I don't want your apology. I want my daughter back home with me."

"It is strange that several of the murders involved your family. Can you think of anyone who hates you enough to—"

"We went over this the last time I was here, and nothing has changed."

"There have been several changes, monsieur. Your daughter is missing, your sister-in-law is dead, and your brother-in-law is missing. It is possible the child is with him."

"Then find him, dammit."

"Where should we look?"

"His home. His job. I don't know. Maybe he's gone back to London."

"London, monsieur?"

"You must have noted that he's British when you spoke to him before."

"His French was quite good, and he never mentioned being a British subject."

"He has dual citizenship. Babbette met him while she was attending university in England. They knew each other all of five months before they married."

"Do you know how to reach his family?"

The father shook his head.

"Wait. Babbette wanted to take Yvette back to London. She thought my daughter would heal better there."

"You of course refused to let your daughter go."

"Oui."

"You had reason to dislike your sister-in-law."

"But not enough to kill her."

FORTY-ONE

Lilliana heard her father's voice echoing in the hallway.

"How charming! Have you run away from home already?"

Lilliana immediately rushed down the steps.

The young boy whom Justin called Felix stood at the bottom of the stairs with Sade's arm around his shoulders. The frightened boy attempted to act at ease but failed.

"Ah, Lilliana. We have a visitor. Or will you be staying?" Sade asked.

"I'm sure he's not staying, although you are welcomed into the house, Felix." Lilliana pulled the boy from Sade's clutches and steered the boy toward the living room.

"What is that child doing here?" asked Marie.

"He's moving in. He can have the room adjoining mine," Sade said.

"Pay no attention to my father and grandmother.

They mostly want to antagonize each other. Sit, and my father will get you something to eat and drink."

"Could you get me a coffee while you're in the kitchen, Louis?" said Marie.

"Grandmother!"

Lilliana startled the boy with her raised voice. "I'm sorry. I'm trying to make you comfortable but am succeeding only at making things worse. Father, do something kind. Get him some soda and cake. That wonderful cake you prepared for dinner. *Oui,* slice him a big piece."

"It's for . . ."

Lilliana's eyes prevented Sade from finishing his sentence. Instead, he turned to head for the kitchen.

"Don't forget the coffee," Marie said.

"If you and Father don't get along better, I will get my own apartment."

"But he and I live for these moments of sarcasm. It really means nothing."

Lilliana sat next to Felix on the sofa.

"Justin didn't come with you?" she asked.

He shook his head.

"I'm glad to see you, but why did you come?"

"I want to live here."

"Why, has Justin done something to you?"

He shook his head.

"Is it because we have a nicer house?"

The boy shook his head.

"Justin hasn't thrown you out, has he?"

He shook his head.

"Then why would you want to live here?"

"Because . . ." The boy's breath halted, and he swallowed deeply. "I like Monsieur Sade."

Marie burst into laughter.

Lilliana attempted to hush her grandmother but finally gave up.

"Felix, I love my father, but most other people don't. He can be abrasive."

"And cruel," Marie managed to add.

"Have you seen our garden, Felix?" Lilliana asked.

He shook his head.

Lilliana took his hand to lead him to the garden. As they passed Sade in the hallway, Lilliana noticed a steaming cup of coffee on the tray he held.

"Arsenic won't work, Father," she whispered.

"But, Lilliana, I've tried everything else."

Lilliana smiled and opened the French doors leading to the yard.

"This is beautiful," Felix said. "We never had a garden in Russia. Too cold." He walked from flower bed to flower bed.

"My grandmother enjoys working out here." Lilliana remained in the shade and watched the boy traverse the entire yard.

"Come, sit beneath the umbrella with me." Lilliana gently beckoned the boy to the seat next to hers.

"Now, let's start over again. Why do you want to live here?"

"Because I like you." He gave her a broad smile. "A lot more than your father and grandmother. They seem sour most of the time, but you're not."

"I don't believe that you want to live with me over Justin. I watched you two together, and you've become very close to each other. I think of you two as brothers."

"He doesn't have brothers or sisters, and neither do I," Felix said.

"You and Justin make a good little family. Why would you want to leave that?"

Felix leaned closer to her and searched the area with his eyes.

"I want to help Justin's mother."

"What!"

Felix hushed her.

"She lives here in a coma."

"A coma."

"*Oui.* Haven't you seen her?"

"I have, but I'm not sure you realize why she lives here."

Felix took several moments to think about this.

"Justin didn't say. But he blames himself. I'm sure he wouldn't have knowingly hurt his mother."

"*Non,* he wouldn't. Let me try to explain the situation. His mother is doing my grandmother a favor."

"While she's in a coma?"

"Justin's mother and my grandmother are extremely close. They're inseparable."

"Then why isn't your grandmother sitting by Justin mother's bed talking to her? I read that is one way to help a person in a coma."

"*Oui.* They have their own private conversations."

"Do you think Justin's mother will ever get better?"

What could she say? *I hope not, because then I lose my grandmother.* That would be the truth, but the boy wouldn't understand.

"I don't know."

"What do the doctors say?"

"The doctors have given up on her, but we haven't."

"May I tell Justin that?"

"*Non.* It makes Justin very sad to think about his mother."

"But he'd be happy to know that you all still care." The boy brightened with the good news he could pass on.

"Let me tell him, Felix. That way he doesn't have to know that you came here by yourself."

"He'd be pretty pissed. Oops, sorry."

"That's okay. I get pretty pissed myself sometimes."

"Shall I decorate the cake with candles and serve it to the young man for his birthday?" Sade asked, standing at the threshold.

"No, I think he'd enjoy having it now out here in the garden."

Sade set down the tray with the cake and soda. He reached a hand out to brush back a curl from Felix's forehead, but Lilliana prevented him from doing so.

"After the cake, Felix is going home to Justin."

"But I thought . . ."

"He's changed his mind."

The boy nodded and took a big bite of the cake.

FORTY-TWO

"Madeline, where do you go?" he asked.

Her brother's face looked troubled.

"I shop for food."

"But where does the money come from?"

"You know I had some money saved."

"Not enough to last this long," he said. He began to look cross. "Are you still seeing Justin?"

"*Non,* but why would it matter if I were?"

"He hates my kind. He'd destroy me if he had the chance. When I was on the streets, the others talked about him. That's how I found you. They all know about you and how much he loves you. That puts you in danger."

"I don't visit Justin. I haven't seen him since the day you showed up at the garret."

"Good. He will die someday."

"I thought the vampires feared him."

Her brother stretched his body, bringing his arms down to encircle her.

"They don't have to fear him, Madeline. He's weak in comparison to us. Too weak to be able to protect you. I will keep you safe from them."

The chill of his body made her shiver.

"What happened to our parents the night the vampires escaped from the cathedral? Did you protect them?"

Her brother stood.

"You blame me because they're dead."

"I want to know what happened. You've never told me the entire story."

He turned his back on her.

"They abandoned me."

"Matthew, they never would have done that."

"You think I would lie to you."

"You misunderstood something."

"That night even the sky caught fire. The heavens blazed, raining smoke and soot on our town. Sparks set my clothes on fire."

She watched her brother hit himself as though he were smothering flames.

"And there were all these ugly beings fleeing through the woods. Many were singed, but some ran as the flesh peeled from their bodies. They screamed, Madeline. Insane screams. I covered my ears with the palms of my hands, and still the shrillness broke through."

"Where were our parents, Matthew?"

"Amidst all the shouts, Madeline, I thought of you and how beautiful you had been when you left the house. I called you a bad name, but I didn't mean it." He turned back to her. "Do you forgive me?"

Madeline smiled.

"You've said worse to me, and I've always forgiven you."

He fell to his knees before her.

"Can we leave Paris?" he asked.

"Where do you want to go?"

"Where I can't hurt anyone." His plaintive eyes begged her for an answer.

"How will we live? Here I can make money."

"The money. Where do you get it?"

"I'm a model for an artist."

"Must you take your clothes off?"

"But he never touches me." She rubbed her hand across his troubled brow.

"He looks at you, though." His voice sounded sulky.

"How else would he be able to sketch me?"

"I should go with you to protect you."

"You can't do that. Once you've learned self-control, then you may come with me."

"I haven't eaten since this morning, and then I merely gnawed on a rat that I found in the kitchen."

"It would be better if you could satisfy the hunger with an animal."

"They smell. They don't taste like humans. Besides, they don't have as much blood." He raised his right hand to touch the pulse on her neck.

"You're getting hungry again."

"I'm always hungry." His fingers touched her pulse and a mist cast a shadow over his eyes.

"I will give you some of my blood if you promise not to take too much."

"I promise nothing." He pulled back his hand.

"Tell me about the night you were changed."

"I've told you. The heat of the fire made me weak; I stumbled several times before I finally fell. A hand touched my arm." He reached out for his sister. "I thought someone would help me stand."

"The hand belonged to a vampire, didn't it?"

"At first the cold hand felt good on my hot flesh. I rolled onto my back and looked at an inhuman face. Its face looked like melted wax. The blurred features lacked expression. Only the eyes told me of the hunger it felt."

"I'm so sorry, Matthew."

"You weren't there. There's no way you could have helped me." He rubbed the palm of his cold hand against her cheek. "I looked down at my arm and saw its flesh oozing across my flesh. With all the strength that remained to me, I rubbed hard, trying to brush the thing's flesh from my own. It burned, Madeline. Initially, he felt cold, but then the flesh seemed as hot as the fire surrounding us. I think it smiled. Hard to tell for sure, but I think it smiled when it saw how upset I was. I rolled away from it, but I couldn't get far enough, because every time I looked up it stood in front of me. Its lips pulled back, showing yellow-green teeth. Still the lips sagged, the skin around the lips melting before my eyes. I've never had a nightmare this terrible."

Madeline's arms ached to hold him. Why couldn't she hold him? she asked herself. Why couldn't she take her brother into her arms? Many times she had hugged and kissed him when he hurt himself. It had been automatic, and should be now.

"Finally, the vampire took mercy and fell upon me. Yes, mercy, Madeline. I see the surprise in your eyes. It smothered all hopes of survival. Suddenly, I understood my fate and accepted it. Only, I thought it brought death, not eternal hell. If I had died there on the ground, God would have accepted my soul. Now I have killed over and over to stanch this hunger that constantly gnaws at me."

"Did you ever see our parents again?" she asked.

Matthew stood. He looked around the decaying room.

"Answer me, Matthew. If you want me to help you, please answer me."

"You can't believe how surprised I was to wake. I lay on the ground. Ants covered my body. I had to strip to brush and swat them from my skin. If it surprised me to be alive, imagine how those ants felt. Their dinner is jumping around, killing off their brethren." He smiled at Madeline. "Don't you think that's funny?"

Madeline covered her face with her hands.

"Do you still want to hear more, Madeline?"

She dropped her hands to her lap.

"Our parents, Matthew. Tell me about our parents."

"It seemed to take forever to get the ants off my body. Finally, I looked down at my clothes and saw the ants infested them. I must go home and get fresh clothes, I thought."

"Why had you left the house in the first place?" she asked.

"To look for you. Mom and Dad wanted me to find you. They were the ones who sent me to Sade's house, only I never got there."

"They shouldn't have. But they didn't understand the danger, I'm sure."

"None of us did. No one really believed in the legend about the cathedral being haunted. Merely a fire had occurred, and they wanted me to bring you home from Sade's party. Did you have fun at the party, Madeline?"

"You know well the horrors that awaited me there, Matthew. It was no different from what you met in the woods."

"Except you survived. You didn't get turned into a vampire, did you? You came away with a hunger for a young man's body, but not his blood."

"Why are you refusing to tell me what happened to our parents?"

"I told you. They are dead."

"How did they die? Were you there? Are they surviving as you are?"

"No, they've gone to God's bosom. The angels flap their wings in happiness to have our parents back. Our

184

GET UP TO 4 FREE BOOKS!

You can have the best fiction delivered to your door for less than what you'd pay in a bookstore or online—only $4.25 a book! Sign up for our book clubs today, and we'll send you FREE* BOOKS just for trying it out...with no obligation to buy, ever!

LEISURE HORROR BOOK CLUB

With more award-winning horror authors than any other publisher, it's easy to see why CNN.com says "Leisure Books has been leading the way in paperback horror novels." Your shipments will include authors such as RICHARD LAYMON, DOUGLAS CLEGG, JACK KETCHUM, MARY ANN MITCHELL, and many more.

LEISURE THRILLER BOOK CLUB

If you love fast-paced page-turners, you won't want to miss any of the books in Leisure's thriller line. Filled with gripping tension and edge-of-your-seat excitement, these titles feature everything from psychological suspense to legal thrillers to police procedurals and more!

As a book club member you also receive the following special benefits:

- 30% OFF all orders through our website & telecenter!
- Exclusive access to special discounts!
- Convenient home delivery and 10 days to return any books you don't want to keep.

There is no minimum number of books to buy, and you may cancel membership at any time. See back to sign up!

*Please include $2.00 for shipping and handling.

YES! ☐

Sign me up for the Leisure Horror Book Club and send my TWO FREE BOOKS! If I choose to stay in the club, I will pay only $8.50* each month, a savings of $5.48!

YES! ☐

Sign me up for the Leisure Thriller Book Club and send my TWO FREE BOOKS! If I choose to stay in the club, I will pay only $8.50* each month, a savings of $5.48!

NAME: _____

ADDRESS: _____

_____

TELEPHONE: _____

E-MAIL: _____

☐ **I WANT TO PAY BY CREDIT CARD.**

☐ VISA   ☐ MasterCard   ☐ DISCOVER

ACCOUNT #: _____

EXPIRATION DATE: _____

SIGNATURE: _____

Send this card along with $2.00 shipping & handling for each club you wish to join, to:

Horror/Thriller Book Clubs
20 Academy Street
Norwalk, CT 06850-4032

Or fax (must include credit card information!) to: 610.995.9274. You can also sign up online at www.dorchesterpub.com.

*Plus $2.00 for shipping. Offer open to residents of the U.S. and Canada only. Canadian residents please call 1.800.481.9191 for pricing information. If under 18, a parent or guardian must sign. Terms, prices and conditions subject to change. Subscription subject to acceptance. Dorchester Publishing reserves the right to reject any order or cancel any subscription.

JOIN NOW!

parents have been crowned with halos that glitter like the stars in the sky."

"Don't be flippant, Matthew. You should be glad if they found true death instead of . . ."

"Instead of living like me. A wretch who will never be human again."

"I won't stop asking you how you know they are dead. Did you find their bodies when you went home?"

"That was a long walk, Madeline. Bodies lined the road, puddles of flesh in the shape of fetuses blocked my way. The fire had diminished, though. I saw smoke in the distance, but the trees surrounding me were either charred or amazingly green with health. I think the smoke in the distance was only dying embers. I never reached the cathedral. I still don't know what that looked like, and didn't care at the time because I wanted to go home."

"No wonder you are so inured to the deaths you cause."

"Inured? That means accustomed to something, doesn't it?"

She nodded her head.

"You think very little of me if you think I've become accustomed to death. I envy every victim I've killed and wish that the thing had sucked me dry instead of feeding me some of its own stench. I do remember that, Madeline. The taste of the thing's blood, or what I suppose passed for blood. Sour. Stale. I imagine acid tastes the same. It burned my gullet. I drank and yet I cried. I drank its blood while it drank mine. It made it oh so easy by opening its own vein and shoving his fist into my mouth."

Madeline almost heaved.

"It was worse than anything you can imagine, Madeline. Remember how we fought not to take the witch's potions when we were sick? You would claw at Mom's steady hand as she slipped the spoon between your lips. And I would hide in the most obvious places, desperate to spare my mouth the awful taste of the witch's brew. Well, those brews were like honey in comparison to the thing's blood."

Matthew leaned over his sister. She smelled his salty, coppery breath mixed with the smell of spoiled meat.

"Do you want to hear more?" he asked.

She pushed on his chest and he fell upon her, knocking her from the bench onto the floor.

"Join me, Madeline, and we can ravage all of France together."

She fought to get out from under him but couldn't.

FORTY-THREE

Madeline lay on the floor looking at the ceiling. He had wanted to frighten her and had succeeded. After nipping her throat lightly with his teeth, he vanished. She couldn't recall when she realized he had let her free. Maybe hours ago, maybe minutes ago.

She reached up to the part of her neck he had bitten, her fingers gently trying to ease the sting. Wet. She pulled away her hand to look at her fingers. Smeared with blood. Her own. Could he someday take her life, or worse, change her into the beast he had become?

Justin, what should I do?

"Destroy your brother" would be his answer. "Free Matthew from the pain he feels," Justin would say.

I can't, Justin. I can't wield a stake into his chest, into his heart.

She wouldn't have to, she knew, for Justin would do it for her. He wouldn't even ask her permission.

What did she think she could do for her brother?

She knew of no way to reverse the change the monster had brought about. For eternity her brother would be a vampire. He'd spend an eternity killing and perhaps even multiplying.

Madeline rolled to her side and attempted to push herself to an upright position, but her arms were too weak to support the heaviness of her body and quickly she fell back onto the spotted wood floor. Her tears blurred her vision, and she thanked God that she couldn't see into the darkness that surrounded her. What if Matthew stood across the room watching her? How could she look into his face? Would his eyes still look merry with the love he had for her? Now his eyes seemed to express only hunger. She imagined his eyes to be like those of people attempting to survive famine.

"Matthew," she whispered, praying for no answer.

Her prayer answered, she wiped the tears from her eyes and looked into the dark corners of the room.

A hat stand tilted to one side. A sheet-covered chair lurked in the shadows. Leftovers from breakfast covered a badly blemished table. The milk carton had been knocked over and dripped its contents onto the floor. He must have bumped into the table on his way out of the room, she conjectured.

The relief of knowing he had left spread through her body. Why did she ask so many questions of him when she couldn't deal with the answers?

She remembered seeing her brother in the doorway of the garret where she lived with Justin. Matthew's wild eyes searched her room to make sure Justin didn't intrude on their reunion. She never hesitated when her brother demanded that she leave Justin and live with him. She loved her brother more than the man she slept with. The siblings had a history that Justin had no part of.

"I love you, Justin," she whispered. "I miss you." But she'd never return to him.

FORTY-FOUR

"Oh, cheer up, Louis. You wouldn't have had much fun with the boy. He looks terribly inexperienced. Besides, Lilliana would have never tolerated your keeping him as a pet."

Sade smirked up at Marie.

"Damn right."

Marie stood shocked at the language Lilliana had used as she walked into the room

"You've been taught better than that, Lilliana. You shouldn't use such coarse language. Tell her, Louis."

"Curse away, *ma chère,* it seems to drive your grandmother mad."

"I'm no longer a child, Grandmother. And you haven't been a delicate lady in a long time. My language is far above the kinds of words I've heard you use."

"Louis, she's insulting me, and it's your fault."

"How so, Marie?"

"She sees how you treat me and thinks she too can

take advantage. I don't think the relationship we have should open doors for Lilliana to disparage me, her grandmother."

"We've all been through too much, Marie, to expect etiquette to reign in this house."

"Another woman has been killed, and all you two do is sit around this house sniping at each other." Lilliana stood with her hands on her hips. "I've gone down to the Seine and tried to obtain information about any wayward vampires."

"Oh, *ma chère,* you haven't been down near those awful, dreary slackers that call themselves vampires, have you?" Marie voiced her concern in a loud voice.

"Don't chastise me, Grandmother. You've wanted me to partake in blood orgies for years. Maybe I should. I could win over the confidence of many of those slackers, as you call them. I fear they simply don't trust me and won't share their knowledge with me."

"I never meant you to become one of those cheap hooker vampires."

"Grandmother, you get most of your blood through the clients that come to you for torture. How can you mock those poor souls down by the Seine?"

"Easily. My victims are all willing. They throw themselves at my feet, begging me to draw their blood."

"They don't know you survive on their blood."

"Yes, they do. They think I survive on the money they give me. In reality, I could donate all their money to charity."

"Then why don't you, Marie?" Sade's dangerous smile caused Marie to halt briefly.

"This is not about money, Louis. This is about the cesspool your daughter has been visiting."

"At times it does smell awful by the Seine. Almost as bad as the mixture of sweat, semen, and blood in your dungeon, Marie."

"Enough," screamed Lilliana. "I want you to get up off your behinds and help me help Justin. These horrid vampires that you speak of know you, Grandmother. And most trust you and Father, or at least fear both of you."

"So, like some low-level gangster, you expect Louis and me to bully these forsaken vampires to tell us all they know."

"Yes. Good analogy, Grandmother."

"Louis, I'm sure you see the ridiculousness of your daughter's request. Send her back into her casket or something."

Sade looked sideways at Marie.

"If I wielded that kind of power in this house, you wouldn't be standing in front of me now." Sade stood.

"Where are you going, Louis? Not down to the Seine."

"No, Marie. I think I'll question Robert and Mark at the brothel."

Marie laughed.

"How will you do that? While laying one of their new arrivals?" Marie asked.

"Neither of you should take this as a joke. We can start at the brothel. The three of us can go there first. Later, we can shift our course to the Seine."

"Louis, tell her we don't want her in a brothel."

"Your grandmother is right. Marie and I will go to the brothel together, and . . ."

Lilliana shook her head.

"Please, how stupid do you think I am? The both of you would get involved in some sort of hedonistic activity, perhaps even together."

Sade groaned.

"And don't look insulted, Grandmother. I've seen you around, glancing and touching Father. There's nothing you'd like more than to finally trick Father into bed with you."

"*Non, non, non,* child. That's not true."

Lilliana folded her arms and glared at her grandmother.

"Besides, I've found a new . . ." Marie hesitated in the choice of her words and finally gave up. "Challenge in Jacques."

"The artist?" Lilliana sounded amazed.

"Yes." Marie stood tall.

"But he seems so easy to seduce. He even offered to give me free lessons."

"What is that cliché?" Sade paused dramatically. "Easy for you but not for your grandmother." He smiled approvingly.

Marie managed to ignore Sade's statement.

"Free lessons? Louis, he's trying to get our baby into bed. I'll have to have a talk with him."

"Don't bother, Grandmother. I've told him no."

FORTY-FIVE

"Lessons," muttered Marie, who had managed to break away from Sade and Lilliana by promising to catch up with them later in the evening.

"Lessons!" she shouted as Jacques opened the door of his studio.

"You want to take lessons instead of posing?" he asked.

"You wanted to give my granddaughter lessons."

"What is wrong with that?" he asked as she steam rolled into the apartment. He stepped over the coat she had dropped to the floor.

"She is my granddaughter. It is obvious you want to seduce her."

"Your granddaughter is beautiful and not a child. I think her love life is none of your business."

"My granddaughter doesn't want to get into bed with a cheap, second-rate artist like yourself."

"She made that clear to me, madame. And you

shouldn't call me cheap. If you recall, you paid a large sum for the statue I sculpted." Jacques dropped down onto his sofa, folded his arms, and challenged Marie.

"I felt sorry for you. It must be difficult for you to make a living."

"Bullshit. If you feel so sorry for me, you'd offer to commission a statue from me rather than demanding I do it for free."

"I must admit that when I purchased the statue I wanted to get a bit of a rise out of my son-in-law."

"Rise, madame?"

"My son-in-law and Madeline had been lovers at one time."

"Alas, everyone seems to be Madeline's lover except for me." Jacques raised both of his hands in the air in exasperation.

Marie sat next to Jacques.

"Don't be so upset. My guess is that she's beautiful but a cold bitch. Can't imagine her warming up to anyone in bed." She passed her fingers through Jacques's hair. "I'm different. I know how to enjoy the company of men."

"Why did you come here, madame? To get laid?"

"Jacques, don't be coarse."

"To make love?" he corrected.

"Get laid is closer to the truth, Jacques. I haven't felt the twinge of love for any man in a long time."

"Not even for this man Louis."

"Louis?"

"You, he, and a menagerie of others appeared at my door not long ago."

"Why would you think I love him? He's my son-in-law."

"It would be awkward for madame. Your daughter may not approve."

"She's been dead for years."

"I'm sorry to hear that, madame. I didn't realize. She must have been very young."

"Younger than me. But tell me, Jacques, what would give you the impression that I want Louis?"

Jacques shrugged.

"There is an aura that seems to circle you both. A tie that won't be broken."

"Yes, there is." Marie became quiet.

"Does madame want to pose for me now?"

"No, Jacques, I want to fuck."

"Afterwards I could sketch out a concept of what I would like to do for your statue."

"There'll be no time, Jacques. Anyway, you'll be much too exhausted."

"You underrate me, madame. While you nap, I shall sketch."

FORTY-SIX

Jacques awoke wrapped around his down pillow. He couldn't remember having wine, and yet the sheet appeared to be spotted with blood. When he moved, his entire body ached. The top bedclothes lay scattered about the floor, and the bottom sheet hung half off the mattress.

"Madame." His voice sounded weak to him. He still felt dreadfully tired.

Each of his muscles screamed out in pain. He rolled over to view the clock. He moaned. It couldn't be that late.

"Maîtresse," he called, remembering the name she had wanted—no, demanded he call her.

Gingerly, he stretched out his legs. At least there hadn't been a dull moment, he recalled.

If he could manage to push his legs over the edge of the bed, perhaps his feet would automatically touch the floor. From there he'd have to depend on what was left of his upper body strength to pull his body up to a seated position.

His legs spilled over the side of the mattress, and the marble floor touching his bare feet jolted him awake. He even found his upper shoulders rising into the air. Seated, he checked the room. Last he remembered, their clothes had been entwined in clumps on the floor. Now only his old jeans and T-shirt decorated the room. His silk briefs had somehow managed to drape themselves on the window latch.

He stood, not straight but slightly bent, his back cursing him for the night of debauchery.

The woman had certainly been out to prove her stamina. He wondered how she had managed to get dressed and leave. If she had left. Perhaps he'd find her drawn and quartered on his sofa in the living room.

Jacques hobbled over to the shut bedroom door, setting his ear to the wood and hoping to hear noise. Nothing. Quietly, he turned the doorknob and pulled the door ajar. Not fully opened. No, he wanted time to straighten his body before she saw him.

In the living room, the morning sun shone through the double windows. A note lay on the end table next to the sofa.

"Maîtresse," he called.

He waited. Several times more he called to her, letting a minute elapse between each word.

Opening the door, he walked into the living room. He picked up the note and read:

Mon chère Jacques,

You were superb. You went far beyond what I had hoped for. I am still so titillated by your desire to please and the skill of your hands, not to mention the most important organ that I must go out and drink some . . .

He noted that whatever she had written here had been heavily crossed out.

"Fluids," she continued. "As tasty as you were, I still need more." He groaned. "But be warned I shall come back for more. Maîtresse."

He dropped the note back on the table and turned toward the bathroom. A warm shower would soothe his sore muscles.

Once inside the bathroom, Jacques closed the door and looked into the full-length mirror. He staggered at the site of himself. Scratches and welts criscrossed his body. Hardly any blood marred his skin. He thought she must have washed him off before leaving in a weak attempt to hide the violence she had wreaked. Slowly, he turned to view his back. He remembered the snake-like whip she had pulled from her oversized purse. At the time, he had laughed to himself, thinking the woman wouldn't have the strength, guts, or know-how to use it properly. How wrong he had been!

He turned on the shower, regulated the temperature, and stepped into the stall. His flesh burned all over. The night's sadomasochistic pleasure replayed through his mind again. She never complained about his rough treatment, and certainly he had to rise to her level of tolerance.

He noticed drops of blood sliding down his abdomen. Several of the cuts had reopened. He'd have to dab a bit of iodine on his flesh to prevent a possible infection.

He closed his eyes and brought his face up to meet the water head-on. The warm spray had started to make him feel groggy again. Quickly, he turned off the hot water and turned up the cold. The chill banished the idea of sleep.

He needed a healthy breakfast and strong coffee. He'd fill the filter this morning and take out the biggest cup in the cupboard.

He hoped that later he'd be rested enough to continue his work with Madeline.

FORTY-SEVEN

"Father, can't you find better things to do with your time? Look at the people walking these streets."

"Lilliana, they are making a living. Not a single one poaches off his fellow man. Each makes, if not an honest living, at least a living."

"Unlike us."

Sade stopped in the middle of the street. Several women knew him by name.

"Lilliana, we don't poach."

"What is it we do?"

"We share our skills with the less fortunate."

"Skills?"

"Prowess at making love."

"Screwing people."

Giving Lilliana a final look of disgust, Sade turned away and continued down the street, nodding occasionally to the hookers who called to him.

Finally, they turned down a quiet working-class street.

"There's a brothel down here?" Lilliana asked.

"Your grandmother found it. She may have even spent some time standing on the very street we just walked."

"She's not here, Father, and I resent your talking about Grandmother behind her back."

"How did I give birth to such a moral child?"

"Maybe it's not in the genes, and there is hope that you can change."

"Blasphemy, child."

Sade led his daughter up the steps to a well-lit town house. He rang the bell and waited only a moment before the door swung open for him.

"We are very happy to see you tonight, Monsieur Sade. There are a few new arrivals that you might like." Robert hesitated but a moment when he saw Lilliana. "There will be two of you tonight." His wide smile brimmed with oversized teeth.

"My daughter," Sade corrected.

"Oh, I'm sorry."

"Not as much as she must be," replied Sade.

"You know that's not true, Father."

"May I invite you both in for a drink?" Robert asked.

"Wonderful. What types of blood are you serving this evening?"

"Father!"

202

"Isn't that what you expected me to say?" Sade looked over his shoulder at his daughter.

"We'll both have champagne," she said to Robert.

Robert led them into the large room with the leather furniture and the well-stocked bar. The bartender had overheard the request and already was popping a fresh bottle of champagne.

"You have a most attractive daughter, Monseiur Sade."

"Her appearance has recently changed."

"A little plastic surgery? So many people are doing that today. We can never be too perfect in how we look."

"Louis." Martin entered the room. "Let me call down our choice treats for tonight."

"Mr. Sade is here with his daughter, Martin." Robert introduced Lilliana.

"Haven't had some good incest here in months," Martin said.

"And you'll have to wait a while longer, Martin, because tonight I've come for information, not carousing."

"I hope you understand, Louis, that we're not a library. We have paying customers that need attendance." Martin stopped the bartender before he could offer the champagne to Sade and Lilliana.

"That is rude, Martin." Sade pushed the little man out of the way and accepted both champagne glasses, handing one to his daughter. "I spend too much money here to be deprived of a simple glass of champagne, don't you think, Robert?"

"Yes, definitely."

Sade sipped his champagne and sat on the leather chair nearest him.

Lilliana tapped Sade's shoulder and said, "Ask them, Father."

"We've come about that troublemaker Justin. You both remember him. You allowed him to abscond with my purchase."

Robert and Martin looked at each other. The smaller man took to the bar.

"Yes, Monsieur Sade. It was a mistake. But we haven't seen him since."

"I have. He still has the boy and refuses to give him to me."

"That has nothing to do with why we're here, Father. Justin is looking for a woman he had been living with. Madeline is her name."

"The redhead. He claims she is honestly a redhead, and we don't have . . ."

"An honest anything here," Martin said, downing the contents of a shot glass.

"Most of the women and men who work here are altered in some fashion. Either it's their hair, their breasts, their noses."

"One or two have even changed the slant of their eyes, hoping to increase their traffic," Martin added.

"That's horrible," Lilliana said.

"We don't necessarily encourage it," said Robert. "And if we do, we pay for it."

"You people are disgusting." Lilliana's eyes opened wide, and the tension in the room grew taut.

"Why, Monsieur Sade, did you bring your daughter?"

"She insisted. Ever since she was a babe, I never knew how to say *'non'* to her."

"Will this Justin be coming back again?" asked Martin.

"For your sake, I hope not," Sade answered. "And now that Lilliana has been introduced to you, I doubt you'll see her again either." He smiled at her.

"Neither of you knows anything about Madeline?" she asked.

"We have no memory of meeting her. I'm sorry. I'm sure it distresses you both to have a friend in such psychic pain."

"Doesn't bother me at all, Robert. My daughter is the one who has taken on his crusade."

Robert turned to Lilliana.

"I am sorry. We only met Justin once under poor circumstances. The woman Madeline we don't know at all."

"Let's go, Father." Lilliana placed her glass on the table next to Sade's chair.

"You know, I might be able to jog Robert's and Martin's memories. Perhaps I'll remain here while you go home."

"I swear, Monsieur Sade . . ." Robert protested.

"My father and I believe you. Father, I am going down to the Seine. We promised to meet Grandmother there. Would you have me go alone?"

Sade placed his glass next to hers and stood.

"You will give our regards to madame when you see her, Monsieur Sade, won't you?" said Robert.

Lilliana huffed her way out the door.

FORTY-EIGHT

"Lilliana and I managed to find our way down to the Seine last night, Marie." Sade found Marie in the garden looking as fresh as the flowers.

"I must have been at the wrong embankment, because I waited quite a while before leaving."

"Your cheeks are flushed, Marie. You look rested and sated."

She giggled to herself.

"Did you have an especially interesting client last night?"

"Client? How could I have kept an appointment with a client? I found myself all alone down by the Seine, barely tolerating those sleazy characters that haunt the waterfront."

"Marie, you never made it to the Seine."

"Louis, I would never disappoint my granddaughter, even though she apparently loves you more than me."

"Grandmother, you're complaining because you

saw me come into the garden. You know I love you as much as Father."

"Not more?" Marie coyly turned her head toward Lilliana.

"Where did you go last night, Marie?" Sade asked.

"I visited Jacques. He knew Madeline, and I thought he might be able to help in our search. But he didn't have anything relevant to say."

"You didn't feed from him, Grandmother."

"Only a slight taste."

"I told you, Lilliana, your grandmother never made it to the Seine."

"Did you frighten Jacques?" Lilliana asked.

"Frighten him? You are so naive, child."

"We might need his help. Madeline may return to him for money or assistance."

"How do we know that Madeline is still in Paris? Maybe she wants to get as far away from Justin as she can. I would," said Marie.

"He's a kind soul, Grandmother."

"He's a vicious destroyer of vampires. He staked his own mother."

"He wanted to end her pain. He didn't know how much worse the other world is." Lilliana grew quiet.

Sade put his arms around his daughter.

"That world is gone, Lilliana. You're here now with family."

"A family that didn't really want me to come back," she reminded Sade.

"I am a coward when it comes to you, Lilliana. I fear

the love I have for you. I know the pain of having lost you once. I don't think I could exist without you again."

"Believe him, Lilliana. I watched him attempt to turn his back on you over and over, but he failed because you were in his heart," said Marie.

The doorbell sounded and sliced deeply into the sorrow that had filled the garden.

"It's the young boy again," Sade cheerfully called out after answering the door.

Lilliana and Marie greeted the boy.

"You've changed your mind again," Sade said, letting his right arm rest on the boy's shoulders.

"No, monsieur." Felix looked at Lilliana. "Justin is talking about a man who has lost most of his family to the Paris killer. Justin wants to talk to the man, but I'm worried."

"Why?" Lilliana asked.

"Because I suspect that Justin thinks Madeline may be the killer."

"Oh, no." Lilliana hugged the boy to her skirt.

"He mourns for her as if she were already dead. I don't want him to find Madeline if it will break his heart," Felix said.

FORTY-NINE

The changes in her brother frightened Madeline. He no longer took to sneaking into the house after a kill. Instead, he strutted. *A bloodstained cock,* she thought. He didn't hide himself away for long hours attempting to cry. His eyes changed to blue-green steel. He stood taller, prouder. He played with his new strength, mangling firm objects in his hands.

"Matthew."

He dropped a crowbar that he had been swiping aimlessly about.

"Oui?"

His eyes now glowed in the dark. He didn't need the weak candlelight to see anymore.

"You've stopped trying to control the hunger. That is dangerous, for eventually you will be caught."

"By whom? Someone like Justin?" His eyes glittered with hate. "I want him to come after me. He took you from us."

210

"I made him take me with him."

"That has always been your flaw, Madeline. You play men against each other."

"That's ridiculous."

"You could have stayed with Sade, but you became tired of him."

"Sade is a cruel man. He hurt me. Justin never did."

Madeline watched her brother's upper lip shape into a sneer.

"You could be with us, Madeline. You could be tasting blood and teaching me how to drink without killing." Matthew raised his hands to show Madeline. "I wouldn't need these nails. I would look normal. I wouldn't have to scratch and rip the flesh of my victims." His hands moved chaotically through the air. "I came to rescue you, and you abandoned me."

"I didn't know you were out that night. I . . ." Madeline thought back to the day of the fire at the cathedral. She could only remember Justin saving her life. Not once on their way to Paris did she ever think of her brother. "I'm sorry, Matthew, I should have returned home. I knew the terror that fled from the cathedral."

"For how long did you know Sade to be a vampire?"

"I learned it only from Justin."

"Justin. I hate that name, Madeline."

"He didn't turn you into a vampire."

Matthew paced the floor.

"Do you still want to know what happened when I got home that night?"

"Please tell me."

"They had the door locked, the windows closed, the curtains drawn. I knocked." He knocked three times on the banister of the staircase to portray what he had done. "Mother peeked from a window. I waved. I tried to smile, but I don't know whether it ever reached my lips. I had seen so much, Madeline. But I instinctively knew that I must look as normal as possible. I didn't want them to be afraid of me, because I needed them." Matthew threw himself down on the bottom step to sit.

"Father opened the door." Remembering how often he had stopped, she urged him on to tell the story.

"Not right away. What does my face look like to you?"

"You look like what you are—my brother."

"No, Mother saw something else. When Dad went to open the door, I heard her protest."

"Fear made her hesitate," Madeline suggested.

"Fear of what she saw in my face."

"*Non,* Matthew."

"Liar!" he shouted, jumping to his feet. "You cower yourself sometimes. It disgusts you to hold me in your arms. Your breath halts as if I smelled like garbage."

Madeline's skin prickled. She wanted to run, but he could run faster. She swallowed, trying to find her voice.

"I smell your sweat, Madeline." His voice came out in a singsong. He walked around her in a circle. Once or twice, he made a move toward her but never touched her.

"You are trying to scare me, Matthew. If you drive

212

me away, who will you have? You don't know how to survive on your own."

"I go down by the water sometimes and hide in the shadows and watch.

" 'Hi, honey, lonely tonight?' they say. 'Can I offer you a treat?' And the mortals fall for it. Sometimes I even see money change hands. I'm learning, Madeline."

"First you must learn self-control. You'll not be accepted down by the Seine if you kill."

Matthew stood very tall, as if insulted.

"Why do you think I hide in the shadows? I'm not ready to join my brothers and sisters yet. But when I am, I won't need you."

"Do you think threats will win me over to your side?"

"You'll never desert me. You would have been like Dad and opened the door. Poor Dad, he wanted me back. He didn't bother to question how I had returned. Poof, the door opens, and he grabs me in his arms. Mom didn't come near us. She stood across the room, staring."

"I don't want to hear any more, Matthew."

"Shall I finish the story another day?"

"I'll never ask you again, Matthew."

"When I choose to tell you, prepare to die."

FIFTY

Lilliana gently knocked on the door to Justin's garret. When he opened the door, she smiled and put an arm around Felix's shoulders.

"We had a visitor, and I decided to walk him home, given how dangerous the streets are."

Justin snatched the boy from her arm.

"I told you to stay away from their house, Felix. You must never go there again."

"But she . . ." Felix pointed a finger at Lilliana. "Is very nice."

Justin looked at her.

"It's okay, Justin. I understand why you wouldn't want Felix visiting our house."

"I don't remember apologizing," Justin said.

"It's in your eyes." She lied. She saw hate.

"Come in," Felix said, pulling Lilliana into the garret. "Justin only keeps beer. Do you want one?"

"No, thank you. Why don't you go bathe and get ready for bed?"

Felix immediately locked himself into the bathroom.

"This is a talk that is not meant for his ears, I assume," said Justin.

"He doesn't know what we are, does he?"

"He's a normal boy, as normal as a boy sold into slavery can be, who happens to live with a half-breed and likes visiting vampires."

"I want to help, Justin."

"I walk the streets night and day now. I'm even planning on intruding on the sorrow of a man who has lost his family."

"Felix told me. He also said that he thinks you fear Madeline is committing the murders."

"The murders started before she left," said Justin.

"And you think she has taken up with the vampire?"

"Why doesn't she come back to me, Lilliana? I know she is alive and still in Paris. I feel her energy. When I visit the scenes of the deaths, I feel her presence."

"At every scene?"

"*Non*, but enough to make me think she knows the vampire. I met a man named Gerard who believes the murders are being committed by a mortal. He thinks the mortal has been rejected by the community of vampires and is now seeking vengeance."

"Do you believe that?" asked Lilliana.

"I know Madeline is not a vampire, but if she kills with a vampire, then I don't have a choice."

"You will kill her?"

"I must kill her and destroy the vampire."

"Why would she suddenly take up with a vampire? Have you asked yourself that?"

"Many times. Is it sexual? Is it some ridiculous romantic notion that she can save his soul? Is it a new-found thrill for her? My mind is about to explode from reasons. That is why I never sleep."

A loud knock shook the door.

"Hide behind the screen," Justin ordered.

"Why?" she asked.

Justin shook his head. "I guess I should be more fearful of who is at the door than you."

The door came crashing inward.

"Cousin!" she cried.

"Cousin? Who is this woman, Justin?"

"Lilliana!" she cried out.

Gerard and Lilliana stared at each other in disbelief.

"You're related to Sade," Justin said to Gerard. "You knew exactly where I could find him and yet you led me on a wild-goose chase."

"Nonsense. Sade and I haven't spoken in years. Besides, you managed to rescue a stray before Sade could despoil him."

"He is right, Justin. Comte de Mirabeau is a distant cousin. They were both imprisoned at Vincennes at the same time."

"*Oui*, my father obtained a *lettre de cachet* on the grounds of filial insubordination. Sade envied my walks in the outdoors there."

216

"My father was too obstreperous to be allowed out-side the prison," explained Lilliana.

"Can't blame him. Vincennes was a dreary place. I have never seen walls so thick, and three moats circled the prison.

"But you claim to be Lilliana," Gerard continued. "She is not mulatto."

"You visited my grandmother several times for money, and when you did, you brought that petulant little dog that drove her crazy."

"I thought she might grow fond of the dog and have mercy on me."

"*Non,* the opposite."

"Damn, I hated the pug-faced thing myself."

"May I ask why you broke into my garret, Gerard? Or shall I call you . . ."

"Gerard is my name now. I can't have people guess-ing that I'm Comte de Mirabeau. Sade takes many more chances than I do."

"And you're here because . . ."

"People are still dying, Justin. And you've not done anything about it. Have you found that damn woman yet?"

"He is trying very hard, Cousin."

"How would you know, Lilliana?"

"Because I'm helping him and Fa—Sade and Marie are assisting."

"The Marquis de Sade doing charity work? I doubt it," Gerard said. "Already the papers are talking of vampires. To most of the journalists it is a joke, but soon they will start believing if these killings continue. Even you, Justin, should worry. As much as you like to deny your vampire half, you too could find yourself tracked down by ignorant peasants like in those horror movies.

"I still . . ." Gerard stopped short. "Who is that?"

All three turned to see Felix standing at the partially opened bathroom door.

"Is that the child you heroically rescued, Justin? He must be very confused by the conversation he just overheard. Boy, come here."

Felix slammed the door shut, and all heard the lock click into place.

"Now you've frightened him, Cousin." Lilliana walked to the door and gently knocked. "Felix, come out and talk with us."

"You'll drink me dry," he yelled.

"Nonsense, boy, we've all had our fill for the day," Gerard said.

"That is not going to bring him out, Cousin."

"Then we shall break in," Gerard said.

Justin stepped in front of the door.

"If both of you left, he'd feel safer," Justin said.

"You have too many distractions, Justin." Gerard grabbed Lilliana's arm and led her out of the apartment.

"They're gone now, Felix."

"That man said you are half-vampire."

"I don't need to drink blood to survive. You watch me eat every day."

"Is Madeline a vampire? Is that why you suspect she may be doing the killing?"

"I pray to God that she's not a vampire, Felix. Before she left this apartment, she was a mortal like you."

"But you think she's changed." Felix's voice sounded sullen.

"I refuse to speak with you with the door shut. Besides, given the fact that Gerard ruined our front door, we have little privacy, and I don't want to yell."

Justin had to wait several minutes before he finally heard Felix unlock the bathroom door.

"I'm not coming in, Felix. You must join me out here."

Slowly, the door opened.

Felix's wide eyes fixed on Justin. He held a plunger and a toilet brush in the shape of a cross.

"Very good, Felix. I see you watch a lot of movies; however, that will not protect you against real vampires. But if it makes you feel more comfortable, then fine, bring your makeshift cross with you." Justin crossed the room and sat on the bed.

"Does the cross have to be blessed?"

"Crosses don't work, period."

"What does?"

"Being intelligent and cautious."

Felix never dropped his arms. He continued to hold the cross in front of him as he walked into the room.

"How did you become a vampire?"

"Half-vampire. My father is mortal, but my mother is a vampire."

"That's why she lives with Sade and Marie."

"It's more complicated."

"Marie is your mother?" Felix lowered his arms, almost dropping the plunger and brush to the floor.

"Sit, Felix. And I'll tell you the whole story."

"How horrible to have Marie as your mother." The boy plopped himself into a chair.

"She is not my mother, but she is using my mother's body."

"That's even worse."

"Everyone in the House of Sade is a vampire. That is why I would not give you to him, and why I don't want you going there."

"Lilliana is a vampire too?"

"*Oui.*"

"Do you drink blood?"

"I don't need blood to survive."

"But have you tasted blood from a human?"

"*Oui.* I'm ashamed to admit that I have."

The brush and plunger fell from Felix's hands. He spent some time collecting his thoughts and then asked, "What does the blood taste like?"

The boy's eyes glittered, his mouth agape with the wonder of his question.

FIFTY-ONE

"I'm sorry, Madeline."

She awoke to the softly spoken words. Her brother's hand touched her shirtsleeve. He patted her arm and kissed her cheek.

"I'm sorry. I didn't mean to frighten you, Madeline. Sometimes something wild takes over, and I'm strong, indestructible. You know I wouldn't . . . hurt you."

" 'Kill me.' You said, 'Kill me.' " She pulled away from Matthew and closer to the wall on the pile of bedding that she used as a bed.

"You didn't leave me, Madeline. Thank you. It took me a long time to find you. I wouldn't want to go looking for you again. And I'd have to, since you're the only person I can trust."

Madeline pushed the blanket off her body and raised herself into a kneeling position. He looked smaller than he had earlier. His hair drooped forlornly over his brow, his eyes had no shine, and his slack face emphasized the bones in his cheeks. But his clothes gave the monster in him away. Splattered in fresh blood, he smelled of death. The fingernails still had the remains of someone's flesh embedded in them. She looked away.

"Please, Matthew, go bathe."

"I disgust you."

"You carry death to my bed, Matthew. Must you advertise what you have done? Couldn't you try to appear human?"

Matthew bowed his head.

"I'm not human. I should be dead." He looked up at her. "Why aren't I dead? Our parents are dead."

"I told you I would never ask you about them again."

"You know what I did, don't you?"

"Go wash, Matthew. Now! Must I drag you into the tub?"

Matthew pulled his shirt over his head and fumbled with the material in his hands.

"Will you buy me another shirt, Madeline?"

"I always do. There are still some clean shirts in the master bedroom closet. We'll have to make do with the jeans for now." She grabbed the bloody shirt from his hands and pointed to the door. "Go. I'll get rid of the shirt."

He didn't move, and she lowered her hand.

"Could you destroy me, Madeline?"

She shook her head and reached out a hand to touch his chin.

"Sometimes I want to run far away from you. I want

222

to forget this ever happened to you. I want to imagine you back home with Mom and Dad, hiding your porn magazines under the mattress, thinking that Mom would never find them."

"They were *Playboy*s, Madeline, not porn." His bottom lip extended into a pout.

She ran her fingers across his lips, and he teased at biting them. They both giggled.

"I guess I should have been smarter than to put the *Playboy* under the mattress. Heck, what an obvious place."

"Are you sure you didn't want Mom to find them?" she asked.

"Why would I want to do that?"

"To rile Mom up. I often thought you purposefully did things to get a rise out of Mom." She smiled. "Mom wanted the perfect house, the perfect family . . ."

"The perfect wealthy husband for you," he said. "That's why she encouraged you to visit Monsieur Sade. She never guessed what he was, and yet she took one look at me and knew instantly."

Madeline pressed her fingers against his lips.

"I said I would never ask."

"I need to tell. Will you listen?"

"You killed them." She could see by her simple reply she had given some relief to Matthew.

"Dad hugged me tight. I couldn't break free. Mom kept staring until Dad called for some clothes for me. She scurried out of the room quickly. I didn't think she'd come back. *Flee,* I told her in my mind. *Flee.*

She must have thought about running, because it took a long time for her to come back with clothes. She came back to help Dad, I'm sure. She knew nothing could be done for me." Matthew smiled. "I never knew Mom had such a long reach. She practically threw the clothes at me."

"You must have had wounds that she could see."

"Only my eyes. Vampires heal quickly. Maybe my breath, too, since I still had the taste of the monster's blood in my mouth."

Madeline buried her head in her hands.

"Don't, Madeline. I need you to listen. Be my priest and hear my confession, because I will never walk into a church again."

She looked at her brother and put her hands on his cheeks to pull him closer. They touched foreheads.

"Mother gave you the clothes."

"I didn't want to put them on. I liked being naked. My body had been so hot in the woods that I couldn't bear placing a stitch against my skin."

"Yet your skin must have been cold."

"*Oui,* that is why Dad called for the clothes. I flung the clothes to the floor, and he chastised me for being indecent. Reminded me that Mom stood in the room. I told him I didn't care. We began to argue, but Mom hushed us. She made excuses for me."

"Do you think she had believed in the vampire legends?"

"*Oui.* I must tell everything to you, Madeline, because the truth will make us closer."

She couldn't understand. Closer? Describing how he killed their parents would make them closer? *No, she thought. Even he knows that isn't true, but he needs to confess.*

"Continue."

He placed his hands over hers. The chill excited her, stimulated her senses. She dug her own nails into his cheeks. He didn't respond initially until she must have done it so hard that it pained him.

"I still bleed, Madeline."

He let go of her hands, and she dropped them from his cheeks. Blood streamed down his cheeks and stained her fingertips. She couldn't turn in any direction without seeing blood.

"Let me get something to wipe your cheeks."

He stopped her from standing, picking up the shirt he had recently discarded. She took the shirt from him and dabbed his flesh.

"We heal quickly, Madeline. By tomorrow there'll be no trace."

"It will still be on my conscience." These words she sincerely meant.

"Be strong for me. Please, Madeline. If God will allow me any salvation, it will come through you."

"We could go to a priest. You don't have to go inside the church. I can bring him out to you."

"I don't think a few Our Fathers and Hail Marys will cleanse my soul. Not even a rosary. And how I hated those long sessions of saying the rosary in church."

"Shh!"

225

"Madeline, He listens to everything we say. He knows what we think. Long ago He knew that I tired of the rosary. And now He watches me kill."

"I can't do this, Matthew. We need a priest. Maybe he can put his hands on you and drive out the demon."

"An exorcism. There's no demon inside of me. Sometimes I wish there were, then I wouldn't be alone or I could hold out hope that the demon would become tired of me. As much as I hate Justin, he is right. My destruction is the only release."

"I'm too weak. I can't . . ."

"That's why I trust you."

"You torture me with your self-pity, Matthew. You see my love for you as a weakness, a crutch for you to lean on. It would be less cruel if you killed me as you did our parents."

"You don't know how they died, Madeline."

"I know you gave them peace."

"Listen, Madeline, listen. Mom and Dad argued over me. She wanted me to go to my room and rest. Dad wanted me to dress immediately. Mom insisted clothes wouldn't matter if I were in my room. She wanted me out of the room, I know, so that she could talk to Dad, tell him about me."

"She only guessed." Madeline shook her head.

"*Non*. Her fear stank. Her eyes displayed panic. The longer they argued, the more stimulated I became. I sniffed their blood in the air, warm, unlike my own. Dad's blood flushed his face, his neck. Veins popped out on his forehead. I wanted to rip the skin off his skull in order to reach the blood that swelled his veins. I didn't stop to think about what would happen to me if I took their lives. Soon I hardly recognized who they were.

"Mom made a move toward me. She wanted to push me into my bedroom, but she couldn't bring herself to touch me. If she had, I might have spared them. I might have recaptured the love I had for them. If she only had taken me into her arms."

"Dad had," she reminded her brother.

"*Oui,* followed by his berating me. 'Do it now!' he yelled. 'Obey me!' I didn't have to obey him anymore. I had the power. I should be the one telling him what to do, I thought. His insults fed the blood hunger inside me. I hadn't tested my strength yet, but I sensed the power growing. I reached out for his throat." Matthew took his sister's throat into his right hand. "I held him steady while he tried to pull away. Mom's screams hurt my ears. Scream, Madeline, scream." He closed his hand tightly around her throat.

Madeline wouldn't cry out, dared not pull from his grasp.

His hand loosened and finally fell away from her neck.

"Filled with shadows, the house throbbed around me. Visions of faces and places flashed in front of me until I managed to concentrate on our dad. His eyes bulged, his mouth opened in a shout, but I only heard Mom. I'm sure she pulled and tugged at me, even hit me, but I didn't suffer any pain. When Dad passed out, I . . ."

"Don't relive this, Matthew. It can't be changed."

"I wanted you there with me. I wanted to blame you, Madeline. I wanted to say to you 'See what your shameless life has done.'"

"You want me to take the blame?" Madeline frowned.

"I want at least to share it."

Madeline went to stand. Matthew pulled her back down.

"Dad sagged to the floor. I wouldn't let him fall. I kept my grip firmly on his throat until he, too, grew cold."

"Didn't Mom run away?"

"She wailed on and on while I coddled Father to my breast. When I lowered my head to him, she must have thought I cried. She came close and screamed again when she saw me trying to gnaw through his skin with my teeth."

Sick, Madeline leaned to her side to relieve herself. Matthew remained quiet until her heaving abated.

"I'm sorry, Madeline," he said.

"*Non*, you're not." She had never felt such anger. "You're testing me beyond what I can bear."

"I want you there with me. Don't you understand? I can't live it alone—only you can imagine the terror they felt. You know what I lost that day."

"Humanity," she said. "You lost any shred of humanity you had."

"And what is happening to you, Madeline?"

"You must want me to go to Justin. Justin is right. You all seek the freedom he brings."

Matthew shook his head.

"I just don't want to be alone with the pain." He went to take her hand, and she pulled away. "Haven't you ever wanted to tell someone about something you did? Haven't you hoped they wouldn't judge you? Instead, you wanted them to cry, laugh, be angry with you. That's what I want from you, Madeline.

"Hear the story to the end. Please."

"I never knew you to be this cruel, Matthew.

"Not cruel. Desperate. Scared."

Madeline leaned back on her haunches, resting against the wall. Her belly ached. Her hands pressed hard against her stomach, trying to take away the flutter that still made her ill.

"Mom tried to run when she saw what I did to Dad. I couldn't believe how fast I moved. Reaching the door before her, I pulled the knob from the door and waved it at her. She surprised me with a knife she had hidden in the folds of her skirt. The knife sliced across my forearms, drawing my blood. Easily, I took the knife from her and slashed at her throat. Blood spurted into the air. A few drops I caught on my tongue. Those drops blurred my vision. When I could see again, Mom and Dad lay white and cold."

Madeline fell forward on to the bedding and sobbed. His hand smoothed back her hair and he kissed her cheek.

FIFTY-TWO

Yvette's father, Jean, walked the streets of Paris, doubting he would find his daughter alive, yet unable to sleep. He found himself climbing the hill leading to the Rues des Martyrs. Here, on the Rue Yvonne Le Tac in the fifth century, St. Denis, decapitated for preaching the Christian Gospel, picked up his head and walked several miles before dying.

Near the Place des Abbesses he stopped at the Notre-Dame-de-Lorette Church to light a candle. He intended to say a rosary. He brought out his black rosary beads and counted out his prayers until his adrenaline forced him to give up. He sat back on the pew and stared at the stained glass windows, the reverent statues all kneeling to God, and the marble and gold meant for royalty.

How many times had he been to church? As a boy, every Sunday. As a man . . . He shyly looked up at the altar.

"Don't punish my daughter for what I've done

wrong. Let the beast on the streets kill me. Let him torture me, but not my little girl."

He weighed the rosary in his hand, torn between returning it to his pocket and flinging it at the altar. At the face of God.

His mother had given him the rosary at his Confirmation. She had even sewn a silk pouch for him to keep it in. The facile embroidery spelled out his name. He slipped the rosary back into the pouch. After kissing the silk, he shoved the pouch back into his jacket pocket. His dead mother would never have approved the fleeting thought he had had.

Before exiting the church, Jean steeped his fingers into the holy-water fount, taking a generous supply for making his sign of the cross.

He passed the butcher shop, the Boucherie Billebault, and wandered down farther to the used-clothing store to window shop. He avoided the antique-jewelry shop where he had bought his wife's engagement ring, instead choosing to browse the art gallery L'Oeil du Huit. He stopped at Le Progrés on the Rue des Trois Fréres for a light meal until the darkest part of night covered the city. As the last customer, he left a hefty tip.

Now he would search for the beast that had taken so much from him.

Did he think he'd find his daughter? Or did he seek a release from this memory-heavy world? The confusion he felt kept him walking. He didn't hesitate when confronted with dark alleys or the rare walker like himself. He noted the others crossed streets to bypass him. The others walked with longer strides and faster gaits. He would stare at passersby who would only allow themselves side glances at him.

Finally, he found himself to be the only person on the street. The houses became shabbier. Many were boarded and burnt out. Eventually, he stopped to listen. The creak of abandoned buildings and the squeak of street rats filled the air. The cobblestone street, vacant of cars, glittered under the moonlight. The smell of garbage floated from the few habitable buildings.

A movement caught Jean's eyes. Had a figure slipped out of the building straight ahead? He squinted, attempting to decipher simple shadow from real life.

He decided to walk closer. Did he want to put his life at risk? Yes.

Would Yvette ever be found? he wondered. The gendarme did a background check on Reginald and found only deceased relatives. The cemeteries of Britain evidently were filled with his ancestors, most of whom died young. Maybe Reginald himself lay dead in the Seine, in a basement with his arms wrapped around the body of Yvette. The cruel visions destroyed his focus. If something had moved, would he have noticed?

The building lay only a few feet away. Nothing moved nearby. Yet a smell overpowered his senses. All the waste of earth and hell existed here. Reflexively, he gagged. Only the beast could give off this stench.

Jean slipped his hand into his coat pocket and fumbled for the rosary. Before he could remove the silk pouch, he found himself thrown to the ground, the air around him impossible to breathe. He tried to reach around, but one of his arms sent a staggering pain through his body, his other arm useless in the blinding blackness of the pain.

The beast rolled off him. Jean managed to turn onto his back. For a split second he watched as a gendarme struggled with the beast. Soon the white face and blind glare of the gendarme stared back at him, blood dripping from his twisted, broken neck.

The small stature of the beast didn't prevent it from throwing the gendarme over its shoulder, easily carrying him away.

FIFTY-THREE

"I see the renegade vampire is becoming bolder. According to the newspaper, he's killed a gendarme." Marie flashed the newspaper in front of Lilliana.

"You shouldn't describe him as a vampire, Grandmother. Gerard thinks it may be a mortal."

"Ripping the throats out of other mortals. *Non, non*, sweetheart, it's a vampire. I have no doubt."

"What do you think, Father?"

"Must you make me agree with your grandmother?" Sade threw his book upon the side table.

"By the way, who is Gerard?" Marie asked.

"A man I met at Justin's garret."

"A loony like Justin," Sade mumbled.

Lilliana remained quiet. *It is better for Father to think Gerard is a loony than know that his despised cousin is wandering around Paris*, she thought.

"Lilliana, we've tried everything to find that poor

fool, his lover. Don't you think it may be time to ignore him? He is rather bothersome to your father and me."

"Grandmother, you don't care what Father thinks or feels."

"Yes, I do." Marie reproachfully looked at her granddaughter.

"Okay, maybe you do when it comes to how Father relates to you. Certainly, you don't worry about how much he is bothered by Justin."

"Louis should treasure the two of us, Lilliana. He has no other living relatives."

Yes, he does, Lilliana quietly said to herself.

"You look guilty, sweetheart. Are you keeping a secret? You haven't fallen for this Justin, have you?"

"With a half-breed! Marie, do you think my daughter has no brains? She merely has a soft heart."

"Hmm. She is keeping something from us, though. You don't want the boy for yourself, do you?"

"Felix! That's absurd, Grandmother. He's a child."

"You were a child when Louis changed you. You were seventeen, as I recall, only two or three years older than that boy living with Justin."

"I wouldn't do anything to hurt him. I just hope Justin could calm him down this afternoon after we left."

" 'We'? This is becoming interesting, sweetheart. I know where Sade spent the afternoon, so you couldn't have been with him."

"You know because you and Father ran into each other at that horrible brothel."

"How would . . . Louis, must you carry stories about me?"

"Lilliana asked me where I had been, and I told her. Your name accidentally slipped out."

"I go there only to counsel the poor women who work there, Lilliana."

Sade broke out into laughter.

"Stop lying to me, Grandmother. I know what your needs are and the places you go to fulfill those needs. I thank you for at least not bringing your activity into this house."

"If you don't want me to lie, don't you think you should be answering my questions truthfully?"

Lilliana looked over at her father. He seemed to have eyes in the back of his head, because he immediately turned to face her.

"I ran into a distant relative today." Lilliana knew they would ask the dreaded question.

"Who?" both Sade and Marie said.

"Comte de Mirabeau."

"That flatulent imbecile," Sade roared. "I thought he died ages ago. I can only hope you saw him lying in state."

"No, he's doing well. He, too, is a vampire."

"I know that," Sade said. "He's the bastard that made me one."

Both Lilliana and Marie stared up at Sade.

"At Vincennes. Your family-oriented grandmother had me jailed on a *lettre de cachet* at the same time as Mirabeau's father had his own son jailed."

"If you remember, Lilliana, the *lettre de cachet* became quite a popular way to rescue wayward relatives. I didn't do anything unreasonable to your father," said Marie.

"Except to jail me and finally have me locked in an insane asylum."

"It didn't harm, Louis. It helped build your character."

"Or lack of character," Lilliana whispered.

Too engrossed in his own fury, Sade did not hear what his daughter had said, but Marie appeared stunned.

"If I run into Mirabeau . . ." Sade said.

"Gerard."

"He's not even brave enough to use his own name."

"Are you? It's contrary and foolish to mark yourself as a person who should be long dead," said Lilliana.

"Tell me, Louis, how did Mirabeau manage to nip you on the neck?"

"Marie, it is your fault, and that is all you need to know." Sade stormed out of the room.

FIFTY-FOUR

Jean had been sitting by his window all day, doing what he had done as a child, watching the clouds drift into a variety of shapes. When a boy, he had lain on his back in the field of his parent's farm and tried to name each formation. Sometimes he'd stare blankly, glad to be safe at home in the French fields. Sometimes he'd fall asleep and would awaken to his dog's kisses.

Now he never slept, and no one brought him kisses. He listened to his neighbors live their lives. He hadn't returned to work himself and probably wouldn't for some time. People had given up intruding on his world, for his melancholy depressed even the young.

The commissariat had wanted a description of the beast. What did he look like? How old was he? Seemed they had ruled out women because of the beast's strength. Would you recognize him again? The only face Jean would recognize is that of the gendarme. People he knew now wore the gendarme's face.

Jean didn't know that the commissariat had assigned the poor man to follow him. Never did the commissariat make clear whether it was for Jean's protection or to catch Jean in the act of tearing someone's throat out.

Jean's broken arm throbbed. The cast made it difficult to do his basic daily activities. Not that he wanted to bathe or bother to dress. Food sat spoiling in his refrigerator and cupboards.

When the knock came to the door, Jean didn't move. *Must be a mistake*, he thought, *or children playing pranks on the weirdo.* The knock persisted until one of his neighbors opened a door. He heard the high-pitched tinkle of the female model next door. The visitor, evidently male, apologized to her. She insisted that Jean had to be home. She had watched him come home. Jean wondered whether she had watched from the window or from the peephole. Occasionally, upon arriving home he would hear the click of the peepholes. His neighbors chose to check on him from afar.

"Jean," the man called through the door while rapping his knuckles hard on the wooden door. His neighbor joined the stranger until his own name sounded like a singsong.

His nerves jangled by the intrusion, Jean stood, walked to the door, undid the locks, and prepared to give the stranger a tongue-lashing. However, when he opened the door a chill passed through him.

"Jean?" The tall, thin young man had flaxen hair to his shoulders, and his eyes literally glimmered.

"I'm sorry, Jean, but this man wanted to speak to you, and I was afraid you might . . ." The model didn't finish her sentence.

Jean stood back, and without being invited the stranger walked into the apartment.

"I'm all right, Genevieve. I had taken a nap and felt groggy, else I would have answered the door sooner."

She looked at him warily, checking for any sign that he may have taken pills and needed his stomach pumped. He smiled to reassure her and closed the door.

"Have we met, monsieur?" Jean turned to take a fresh look at his visitor.

"*Non*. My name is Justin. I read of your experience with the killer in the newspaper."

"You came to see what a survivor looked like?"

"I need your help."

Jean raised his arm at Justin.

"I was no help to that poor man protecting me." Jean indicted a chair. "Pull the chair up to the window and sit by me. I like the daylight, the noises, the smells, the rumble of the world being busy." He sat. The visitor unnerved Jean when he picked out the weighty chair and carried it so lightly to the window.

"You are stronger than you look, monsieur."

"Please, my name is Justin." He sat across from Jean.

"Do you also want to know what the beast looked like?"

"The beast? Oh, you mean the killer."

"Having seen what he can do, I feel correct in calling him a beast."

240

"Than it was male, not female?"

Jean saw Justin lean forward, awaiting the answer.

Jean shrugged. "I don't know. I don't know of any woman that strong, or of any male who could flee so fast without effort. Maybe it was an animal. Do you remember Poe's story about the Rue Morgue?"

"I spend very little time reading."

"I read all the time to my children. When they were young they would request stories, sometimes the same ones over and over until it became tedious. Older, they showed more interest in diversity. I was sure that they would go on to higher education, unlike me."

"You still have a daughter," Justin reminded.

"She is missing. The police have kept it out of the papers. No body, no reason to upset the populace."

"I wish I could do something for you, Jean."

"Find the beast. He may still have Yvette. I sound foolish, don't I? Dreaming about a daughter that has been missing for days. You probably read about Babbette's death. She took Yvette from school the day she died. I had to identify Babbette for the gendarmes. She had the same look as the gendarme assigned to watching me. The medical personnel hadn't even bothered to close her eyes. It was the one and only good thing I ever did for Babbette."

"Where did you encounter the killer?"

"In a practically deserted neighborhood. The gendarmes are positive that I had been contemplating suicide. To be honest, I don't know whether I wanted to die."

"You must keep yourself safe for Yvette," Justin said.

"What if she never comes back, Justin? What if her body is never found? Should I go through life looking into faces, hoping that somehow she had escaped and still existed on this earth? When do I give up?"

"Why give up? You have been spared for a reason."

"Another man died in my place."

"Don't waste his death."

FIFTY-FIVE

Justin walked home with the information he had sought. Also with a new reason to give up his search for Madeline in preference to finding the killer.

Half a block away from his house, he spied Marie talking to Felix. He quickened his step, eager to drive the woman away from his charge.

"Felix," he shouted.

The boy ran to him, leaving Marie with a look of dismay.

"What have you been telling the boy, Justin? He thinks I'm a creature of the night, and here I stand under this bright spring sunshine."

"He explained to me how hokey all those movies are," the boy said.

"They're more than hokey, boy. They are bad publicity." Marie bared her teeth and lunged at Felix, who ran immediately up the steps of the house.

"You've managed your fright for the day, Marie. Anything else you wanted to do?" Justin asked.

"That boy is dreadful, accusing me of incredible actions. He wanted to know whether I was old and ugly, and whether that was why I stole your mother's body. Must you go around telling stories behind my back?"

"If you had been present the day I told him, I would still have told him everything."

"How did the topic come up, anyway?"

"Your cousin Mirabeau paid me a visit."

"Louis's cousin. I wouldn't go near Mirabeau myself. I understand he now calls himself Gerard."

"Doesn't matter what he calls himself. He carelessly spoke in front of Felix."

"Amazing that he's managed to survive. But tell me, Justin, why have you and he become friends?"

"We aren't. He wants my help in stopping the serial killer. He feels the murders might reveal the fact that there are actually vampires."

"He does have a point. Tell me, have you found Madeline yet?"

"*Non.* The serial killer must now be my first task. If I continue to go in circles looking for Madeline, too many people will die."

"I wish I could help; however, Jacques is so tight-lipped. I can get no information from him."

"Even if you did, Marie, you wouldn't tell me."

"I'm sorry you won't give me another chance, Justin. Don't you think I'd tell you where you could find Madeline, at least so my granddaughter wouldn't be obsessed with your problem? Have you two been spending a lot of time together? She mentioned being at your garret."

"Lilliana is beautiful and not at all like you, but I have no interest in spending an excessive amount of time with vampires."

Marie huffed.

"You think she isn't good enough. Fine. I should be grateful you feel that way. She is a good girl. It would help if you told her that you don't need her help anymore."

"Find Madeline and I won't need any help."

FIFTY-SIX

"Jacques, is this work you're doing with Madeline very important to you?"

"Please remain still, madame, and keep your mind on what we are doing."

"You're doing something. I'm lying here bored to death."

"The expression. Your facial expression. You're in ecstasy, overcome by the purity of all that is dear to you."

"Nothing pure is dear to me, Jacques. I could do with a good fuck right now." She sat up, her breasts jiggling playfully under the light of the sun.

"*Non, non,* madame. I am at the most crucial point in my sketching. Don't ruin the moment when the muse is sitting on my shoulder."

"Dandruff is the only thing sitting on your shoulders, Jacques. Besides, I need to stretch." She stood and circled the room. "Do you think the smell of all the paints you keep might be eating away at your brain?"

"Madame is doing everything she can to break the mood."

"No, I'm serious. The paints have no effect on me, but I worry about you, Jacques."

"Let my mother do that," he said.

"Wouldn't you like to live forever and not worry about the dreaded diseases that multiply every day?"

"I think it is better if you and I don't live forever, madame."

Marie came up behind him and settled her hands on his shoulders.

"I have a secret, Jacques, that I might share with you."

"Please don't, madame. If the secret should be revealed, I'd be the first you'd blame." He shrugged one shoulder to kiss her hand.

"My flesh is like ice, isn't it?"

"In bed it can add to the sport."

"I like you, Jacques—you set no boundaries in bed. Makes me feel cared for."

"As long as you never mention the word *love*, we can agree on most everything else, madame."

She rubbed against him.

"What did I ask you to call me?"

"Maîtresse." He grinned, lifted his charcoal pencil, and began to draw on Marie's flesh. He drew Marie as a dominatrix wearing only net stockings and high boots.

247

"I have them, you know. The boots. The stockings."

He switched pencils and colored red circles around her nipples.

"Tickles, Jacques." She undid the buttons on his shirt. Setting her tongue to his nipples, she laved them until he shivered. She ran her fingers through the curly, dark hair on his chest and stretched her body to touch her tongue to the tip of his nose.

"Who should play the top this afternoon, Maîtresse?"

"I always do, Jacques. We play my game. No one has ever complained."

"We both can say the same." Jacques removed his shirt. "Unzip me."

"*Non*. Say please?"

He took her hands and laid them on the zipper. She snapped open the button and gradually slid the zipper down.

"Remove them," he demanded.

Her hands slid the denim over his hips, down his thighs, and he watched as the material gathered at his feet.

He stepped out of his jeans and used a bare foot to kick the jeans away.

Her fingertips played across his underwear, outlining the large organ straining to be released.

"Take the rest off, Jacques."

He shook his head. "Wait. Go back over there and pose."

"Hell, I'm . . ."

Jacques placed a hand over her mouth.

"Do what *I* say, and then I'll gift you."

"Otherwise?"

"You'll be using your vibrator tonight, Maîtresse."

"At least let me savor your dick with my eyes. The look of ecstasy might be easier for me to produce."

Jacques spread his arms wide.

She knelt before him. Her fingers dragged the tight material down over his penis and let the underwear fall to the floor. While moving her head forward, she grasped his thighs, but he stopped her from taking him fully into her mouth.

"I will fill every hole you have once I judge that you've labored enough for it."

Marie stared at the trundle bed across the room and obeyed.

FIFTY-SEVEN

Early the next morning, Marie left Jacques's studio sated by his blood and sexual acumen. She'd give him a few days to replenish before visiting again. The black veil on her irritated her chin, but afraid that she looked too wild, she kept her face hidden.

She mounted the steps to her house and stopped at the door to select the proper key. About to slide the key into the hole, she suddenly felt a chill.

"Marie, I didn't run into you last night. I thought perhaps you spent the evening with your granddaughter."

"Don't startle me, Louis." She slid the key into the hole and quickly twisted the lock. Upon opening the door, she meant to climb the staircase to her room, but Sade stopped her.

"You're very quiet, Marie. It's rare when you're not up to a bit of verbal sparring."

"My coffin is calling to me. The long night drained me," she said.

"Come, Marie, you are the one who does the draining." Sade chuckled. He caught hold of her forearms. "What is this? Bondage marks on *your* wrists?"

"Are you jealous, Louis?"

"You played the submissive, Marie. How unusual."

"The marks will vanish after I nap." She tried to pull away from him. "Do you have something else to say, Louis?"

"I am overcome with awe. I would never have believed you'd allow someone to tie you down. Male? Female?"

"Talented," she answered.

"You've been posing, haven't you? The sculpturer Jacques is the one who did this," he said, holding her wrists up into the air. "What else have you permitted?"

"A fuck."

"You are always up for that, Marie. No, what other dangerous activity did you engage in? What marks would I find on your body?"

"You've never been interested in seeing my body before, Louis."

"This body you've stolen is far more attractive than your original ancient sagging flesh."

"Why haven't you taken me up on my invitations?"

"Because your body is attractive but you aren't." He let go of her wrists. "You've given Jacques a lot of territory to explore."

"Even when bound, I'm stronger than he. The game is not unsafe."

"You're not playing a game, Marie." Sade pulled off her veil with her hat. "Bites?"

"He became too enthusiastic."

"And you let him? Or did your spirit weaken and allow him to dominate over you?"

"Why do you care? Has jealousy warmed the cockles of your heart, Louis?" She reached for his chest and moved closer. "The night doesn't have to be over."

Sade sneered.

"You smell, Marie, not just from Jacques's semen and touch, but from your own withering pride. You think I would want to revisit the territory Jacques explored last night? Look at the bruises and welts? You're much too damaged."

"Unlike the prostitutes you visit? I can smell their cheap perfume on you, Louis. How about lipstick smudges on your collar?" Marie attempted to examine his shirt.

"You'll only find blood, I'm sure." He batted away her hands. "Perhaps a bit of sweat that rubbed off when the prostitutes worked hard at satisfying me."

"Sorry you're having problems climaxing, Louis." She turned to go up the stairs but hesitated before turning back to Sade. "What, no reply? You must be having serious problems."

"You know what you say can't be true, Marie. You merely want to rile me. I'll never bed you to prove my virility."

"Then I shall always doubt it."

"You are wrong about so many things that I've become bored with trying to correct you. Hurry upstairs to your coffin, Marie. There's nothing or no one to keep you from it."

"Least of all you, Louis. Why should I waste my time with a man who is almost a eunuch?" Marie stripped down to bare skin. "Look at the bruises, Louis. Each one made me moan. I wished for every blow and for every gentle soothing touch that followed. Soon he'll feed as I do. He'll sleep my sleep. And he'll beg me for the right to do so."

"Careful, Marie. Not everyone understands our life."

"Death, Louis. Our death."

"He may refuse your blood," Sade said.

"He gave me his freely, intrigued by the nibble on his flesh, the rush of his blood into my mouth, and the dizzying spell that follows."

"Don't go back to Jacques, Marie."

"Why not? Because you've finally come to your senses and realize what you've been missing?"

"I look out for your safety because of Lilliana."

She saw his eyes grow dark, saw the storm gather in them. He shocked her by bending over to pick up her clothes and handing them to her.

"If Lilliana should come down, she shouldn't see you like this."

"Yet you whittle away at my character in front of her. I don't need clothes to maintain my granddaughter's love. She loves you, and I certainly have never done anything worse than you. Call her down and ask her."

"You're drunk on your lover's blood."

"*Non,* Louis, I've merely found a mortal to equal myself. Burn the clothes. Or give them to your strumpets that you prefer over me."

"This isn't going to change my mind, Marie. I'll not bed you."

"I don't need you to. Within the next few weeks, I'll have a mate for eternity."

"Your love can't last that long, Marie. Don't foul this house with one of your blood victims, because I know you'll grow tired of him."

"It's you that I've grown tired of, Louis." She marched up the stairs, conscious of her body movements. She knew Sade would stand at the bottom of the steps watching her toned muscles and creamy flesh ascend.

FIFTY-EIGHT

Justin followed the directions Jean had given. The worn streets needed repair, but most of the houses waited for demolition. The few people on the street begged for money. The dogs cowered while rats took over the streets at dusk. Jean had been vague about the description of the house from which the beast had come. Jean said the house looked abandoned, perhaps even boarded up, but many of the houses on these streets had wooden boards blocking windows and doors.

He noticed a bloodstain on the ground and realized this had to be the spot where the attack took place. Both houses in front of him stood empty, the boards barely clinging to window frames. Nails rusting from the rain weakened, letting boards slowly drift toward the ground. The crumbling stairs leading to the front doors sloped downward.

Did he expect to come here and find the beast sitting on one of the terraces waiting for him? No, but he did hope he could attract the beast out of its hiding place.

Madeline checked out the top window of the house for her brother. Instead, she caught sight of Justin staring at the front door to her house. She peered through a wide crack in the boards, her hands resting against the rough hardwood.

"Justin," she whispered, although she wanted to shout.

She could run from the room, down the stairs, and swing open the front door. He'd rush to her, she knew. He'd take her back. He'd . . . What would he do or say when he learned of how she had abetted her brother?

"Justin." The soft sound of his name brought her a measure of peace.

He squatted down to touch the blood on the cobblestones, and Madeline wept not for the dead gendarme and not for her brother. She wept for Justin, for now she understood his pain. She understood the quest he had taken on when he declared he wanted to bring peace to the undead.

"How brave you are, Justin. I'm too weak to end my brother's pain."

Justin stood and seemed to be trying to select a deserted house to enter. If he found her here, would he force her to leave her brother? Need she mention her brother? Why had she taken shelter in an abandoned building? She had no answers.

But Justin had a kind heart and loved her too much to judge her. His mother had been a vampire. He knew how love prevented a person from acting morally.

She looked behind her at the door. Matthew had been gone for almost two hours. She had no idea when he'd return, and she knew someday he might not come back to her. Not that he'd desert her, no, but one day he'd be forced to pay for his misdeeds. What would she do then? Search for Justin? Crawl back into his bed and hold him tightly while her nightmares pursued her night after night?

She looked back out the window and noticed he had moved closer to her house but stopped short of climbing the steps.

A sound drew her attention from him, and she pressed her forehead to the window to see the shadow dogging Justin's steps.

Justin heard a jerking tread coming closer, the feet softly hitting the ground in order to surprise him. He waited before swinging around with a closed fist to hit the being behind him. The interloper fell on the blood-stained cobbles.

An elderly man raised his head, and Justin watched the man's eyes try to focus. After a few shakes of the head, the elderly man stared directly at Justin.

"One of those gawkers, aren't you? Come around to see how the poor live. Makes you feel better about your own life. What do you do? Pick up garbage? You don't look like any professional. Your shoes could have been bought at a secondhand shop. Maybe it's a disguise. You want to pass as one of us. Think you're safe that way, otherwise you think we'll rob you."

"Old man, what are you doing on this street late at night? A gendarme died here the other night."

"You mean by that serial killer that's been roaming the city. He'd do me a favor if he put me out of my misery. People like me don't get killed. The dark fates watch over me. They make sure I suffer my hell here on earth. They won't cut my agony short."

"Do you have family?"

The old man rolled over, drawing himself up onto his hands and knees. Justin rushed forward and helped the old man rise to his feet.

"Got myself a woman," the old man said.

Justin looked around.

"She's laying back in the rubble we call home. Been drinking too much. Been sick, too. I couldn't take the smell, so I decided to get some air." The old man took a deep breath.

"Shouldn't you be back watching over her?"

"What for? Think I'd be able to wrestle with this killer?"

"You were going to try to wrestle with me," Justin said.

"I hoped I could knock you out with this hammer." The old man bent down and picked up a small black hammer. "Before it came to hand-to-hand combat."

"What did you expect to get for the effort?" Justin

asked, emptying his pockets to show what little money he had. "Here, take it."

The old man grabbed the few euros. Justin instantly took the hammer from the old man.

"Hey, that's how I make my livelihood," the old man complained.

"By hitting innocent people over the head?"

"Nah, I do carpentry when I can see straight."

"Then mugging people is a hobby."

"Drinking is my hobby. Mugging helps to pay for the hobby." The old man smiled; his teeth, chipped and misshapen, filled up his small mouth. "Why are you walking this street? Curious about the color of blood? I saw you kneel down and touch those cobblestones. This isn't a shrine for praying."

"I'm looking for the killer."

"You're not a gendarme. Must be some kind of weirdo." The old man spoke the last sentence in a low voice to himself.

"Were you near here when the gendarme died?"

"I think I saw that man who's looking for his child. He's never going to see her again. Some pedophile is having a good time with her."

The old man began to laugh, but Justin's fist cut it short.

Justin thought he heard a female yelp, but he had been so focused on the old man that he couldn't be sure. He looked up at the houses that circled him. No one stood at a window, but he could not tell for sure, since the blackness inside the buildings could be used for cover.

"*Merde!* You broke my nose," the old man yelled.

Justin looked down and saw that the old man's nose bled but didn't look broken.

"You going to take me to a damn doctor or leave me in the street here for that killer to find?"

"Old man, I'll help you to your feet, and you can find your own way to a doctor."

"What, with the stingy amount of money you gave me? I can't walk. I'll need a cab."

"I don't have any more money."

"Cheap bastard." The old man attempted to stand, but his legs buckled from under him.

"Let me help you." Justin pulled the old man to his feet. "You're not really sober yourself, are you?"

"I never said I was." The old man's legs refused to carry his full weight.

"I'll take you to a hospital," Justin said.

Madeline watched Justin lift an old man into his arms. She hoped Justin hadn't done any serious damage to the old man. She knew the old man from the neighborhood, always cantankerous, always ready to take advantage of another's generosity.

"Is he still out there, Madeline?"

She turned back toward the door to see Matthew filling the space before her. Nothing else existed in the room but the two of them.

"It's just old Pierre," she said.

260

"No, I mean Justin. I saw him before I walked down the street. Vampire eyes are sharp, you know. At first I thought you had sent for him, but he walked too slowly and didn't know which house to choose first. I figured you would have greeted him at the door if you had asked him to join us."

"You killed close to home. What did you expect, Matthew? Of course people will be snooping around here."

"Not for long," he replied.

She knew he must have killed another victim in a distant area of Paris, partly for blood, partly to throw the scent away from where they lived.

He walked toward her. When he reached the window, he needed to stand on tiptoe to see out the crack in the wood.

"He's taking old Pierre home. Nice of Justin, isn't it? Nice of Pierre to show when he did. Imagine what the confrontation would have been had Justin entered our home."

"Don't harm Justin."

"More likely he'll drive a stake through your brother's heart. Doesn't that worry you more?" He looked her in the face. "Answer me, Madeline. Don't make me think you have doubts about us staying together."

"Sometimes I wish you'd ask to be destroyed," she said.

"Then the situation would be easier for you, wouldn't it? I'll never do that. I have nowhere to go after this life."

Fifty-nine

"I'm glad you came today, even though I know it must be for the money, not for my company." Jacques soaked his hands in water before shaping the clay. "Madeline, I wish you'd think better of me."

"What am I supposed to think? I already know you have many women who leave various mementos for you to treasure until their next liaison with you."

"Why must you women savage a man's house searching for clues to what he is doing while you aren't there?"

"I don't search. You're a careless housekeeper and should know women leave personal items as a way to stake out their territory. Earrings, face powder, a lipstick, or a thong," she said, lifting a hot-pink bit of material from the floor.

"Of course women take off their clothes here. They are modeling for me."

"Even your students strip naked, Jacques. Is that to make them feel uninhibited while they create?"

"Exactly," Jacques said, wondering why he had never thought of that line before. He dried his hands quickly on a towel and unbuttoned his shirt. "Clothes restrict movement."

"Don't, Jacques. If you take a stitch off, I will leave."

With only one of his shoulders free of the shirt, he hesitated.

"I mean it, Jacques. I'm modeling because we need the money, not because I want to sleep with you."

He shrugged back into the shirt and soaked his hands in the bowl of water again.

Jacques hadn't seen Maîtresse in several days and hoped she'd show again after he finished his work with Madeline. At least Maîtresse didn't want anything from him, unlike the younger girls that seemed to almost require his blood. He smiled to himself, thinking about the last time Maîtresse had been to his studio. She had taken his blood, but only literally. He knew she left him his soul to find his pleasures elsewhere.

"This man that you support must be very talented in the art of lovemaking." He waited to hear her protest or nod. Neither happened. "Many times you would talk of Justin, but you never mention this new man. Why, Madeline?"

He received a stony silence.

"How did you meet him?"

263

Madeline didn't flinch.

"I'm asking because you hate modeling for me. I can tell, and not just because you won't make love. Your body is rigid. Your face lacks expression. Yet you sit for hours like a martyr. You never even ask for a break. I become tired and bored before you do."

"Then why go through this charade?" she asked.

"Because you need money, and I'll not gift it to you. You must pay as you paid for the lessons."

"That is fair, Jacques."

"Won't you share anything with me, Madeline? If you did, you might not have to pose. I could help you if I knew what you were up to."

"Finish your work, Jacques. It is better you don't have any connection to my life. You would be frightened."

"Are you frightened, Madeline? Is that why you tell me nothing?" He stopped working to study her face. Without her great emotional strength, she would be crying now. He could tell by the shine her eyes had taken on. "Is he cruel to you?"

"*Non,* you are!" she yelled, jumping from the table on which she had been standing. She rushed for the door to his bedroom, where she had taken off her clothes.

"I'll never tell Justin," he muttered to the empty room. "Never."

A few minutes later, he saw her flash by the studio, and seconds later the front door slammed shut.

SIXTY

Gerard crossed the avenue, feeling oppressed by the muggy Paris night. He circled the block several times before stopping at Sade's home. The house appeared normal. Lights lit half the house. Several window boxes decorated the first-floor windows. Most of the plants had fresh blossoms. The filmy curtains on the windows allowed a passerby to occasionally see a shadow, but no more than that.

He dreaded climbing the steps to the front door. He hadn't seen Sade since Vincennes more than two centuries ago, but Sade held grudges much longer than most men.

Should he face Sade or . . . ? He didn't have a choice. Justin didn't spend enough time tracking down the serial killer. Instead, the idiot ran after a woman who had probably already forgotten about him.

With a determined gait, he climbed each step. At the door, he paused only briefly before slamming the knocker hard against the door. It took but a few moments for a woman to answer. Attractive, he thought, and definitely vampire.

"Is Monsieur Sade at home?" he asked.

"Comte de Mirabeau! Wonderful to see you. Lilliana mentioned meeting you at that creep's place."

"Creep, madame?"

"You might call him Justin."

"Ah, *oui*. And you are, madame?"

"Of course—you don't recognize me either. Lilliana explained how it took a while for you to fully accept her physical changes. I guess I'll have to explain it all over again."

"Lilliana said . . . You are Marie!" A rush of excitement overcame him when he realized that he may be speaking to an ally.

"Come in. Sade isn't here, but I can find a way to entertain you." Her eyes narrowed and one eyebrow rose.

"Thank you for inviting me in, Marie. Perhaps it's better that I speak to you first."

She led him into a well-furnished room with notable antiques prominently displayed.

He sat upon a maroon velvet love seat that he could have sworn he had seen a century and a half ago in a brothel.

"Booze?" she asked.

"A touch of brandy."

"I suppose Lilliana has filled you in on what she and I have been doing."

266

"And what Sade has been up to. The cathedral incident was regrettable."

"Wasn't all Sade's fault." She gave him a balloon glass one-third filled with brandy. "That horror Justin really caused most of the fuss."

"Sade should have known that someday he would have to deal with those he had locked in the cathedral."

Marie shrugged.

"Marie, I'm here because I wanted to ask Sade whether he is the serial killer."

Marie chocked on her gin and tonic.

"Sade? Sade and I have learned to take a touch of blood, and we've figured out a way to make people want to give us their blood. Neither of us would foolishly drop dead bodies all over Paris."

"He's done other foolish things, madame."

"Has Justin put this idea into your head, Comte?"

"Lilliana did when she filled me in on what your family has been doing over the years. Initially, I had thought the killer to be human. I had forgotten how Sade liked to advertise his bad habits."

Marie sat back in her chair and closed her eyes.

"And what if he were the killer? He wouldn't stop because you asked him to, you certainly know that."

"I'd enlist help in destroying him," Gerard said.

She opened her eyes and stared into Gerard's.

"And who would be brave enough to assist you?"

"Honestly, I'm delighted to know you are living with Sade."

"You mean that I have access to Louis." She took a deep swallow from her drink.

"We both have always been aware of his faults."

"You don't want to do the dirty work of destroying Louis because you made him what he is."

Her knowledge surprised Gerard. Perhaps this mother-in-law son-in-law relationship had cemented more over the centuries.

"Did he give you details?"

"No, but they must be interesting, because he seemed quite pissed off. He made me, you know."

"Not willingly, I'm sure." Obviously, Marie had taken these words as an insult, for she puffed up immediately. "I only say that because you and Sade did not have a good relationship. I never thought he wanted to accept your company for eternity."

"You want me to stake Louis?" she asked, rising to her feet.

"He is your maker, and I believe you would find it difficult to do because of that."

"There isn't much I can't do. Besides, who else would help?"

"Justin."

Her sarcastic chuckle displayed the disdain she had for the young man.

"I would have gone straight to Justin, except he's been lax in searching for the killer. He has killed many of his own kind. I don't think ridding the world of Sade would be too emotional for him."

"It might be too complicated for him, though. He

isn't the cleverest of men. He's morose and obsessed right now."

"You mean about the woman Madeline?"

"An ex-lover of Louis's."

"Justin told me. Does Sade know where she is?"

"*Non.*"

"Are you sure? If Justin got her back, he would be able to put his mind into destroying the serial killer."

"Louis?"

"I'm only suggesting. I have no evidence. If Justin could find Sade in the act, Justin wouldn't hesitate to destroy him."

"Justin certainly wouldn't pause for a moment if he thought Louis meant to kill Madeline."

"I came only to confront Sade, not to set him up. I want the real serial killer destroyed, madame."

"Maybe Louis is the real killer." She paced the room. "Louis tolerates me only because of Lilliana. I've tried to repair our relationship. Eagerly, I offered him a way to draw us closer to together. The damn fool refuses. A few days ago, he took to cruelly insulting me. Refusing to accept my sculptor friend into his home. Can you imagine—I live here as though I were a poor relative."

"Why not move out?"

"Because I want to be near Lilliana. We lost her, and now that we have her back, neither Louis nor I wants to give her up."

"I'm sorry about your situation, madame, but it has nothing to do with the reason I'm here."

She swung around to face him.

"You want Louis destroyed."

"*Mais non,* I want the killer destroyed."

"They may be one and the same."

"I know, madame, that you and Sade have had a long, angry relationship. It must be difficult for you to live under his conditions. However, I trust that neither of us would want to see harm come to Sade if he is innocent."

Marie laughed.

"I doubt Louis could have been innocent even as a boy. He probably tortured animals as a hobby. Only Lilliana would miss him."

"Then you certainly can't be part of this investigation." Gerard stood. "I'm sorry I bothered you. For Lilliana's sake, I will leave now." He turned to go.

"Thank you for coming," she said. "You've given me a wonderful idea to teach two annoying pests a lesson."

Gerard regretted visiting the house. Venom still polluted the air between Marie and her son-in-law, making him feel unclean—and worst of all, part of a twisted plan that he never meant to help hatch.

Sixty-one

"Jacques, when does Madeline come for her sittings?"
Marie's tongue circled his right nipple.

"It shouldn't matter to you," he answered. He felt her teeth prick the nipple. "Ouch! Haven't you drawn enough blood from me today?"

She used her right index finger to dip into the drop of blood swelling from the nipple.

"Open wide, *mon amour*." She rubbed her index finger on his tongue. "Do you like the taste of blood?"

"I've wondered why you do. How did you come upon this unusual habit you have?"

"Many years ago. Seems like centuries actually. Would you like to try drawing blood from me?"

He scrunched his face into a sour grimace.

"I'll leave the bloodletting to you, Maîtresse. I prefer wine." He took hold of a glass of wine on the nightstand and downed what had been left.

"You might change your mind one day. There are benefits to drinking from me."

Jacques pushed her aside and sat up in bed.

"Let's not talk about such things, Maîtresse. I get chills contemplating what could be going on in your mind."

She rolled over onto her back.

"Let's talk about Madeline. I'm sure she gives you a different kind of chill. One far more enjoyable."

"You are fixated today. You've spent most of the morning asking me about Madeline. Have you decided to tell Justin that she comes here to sit for me?"

"We have a pact. Do you doubt my ability to abide by it?"

"Why would you want to see her again?" he asked.

"The opposite. I want to be sure not to run into her."

"I can manage that, Maîtresse."

"Every time I come here I hold my breath at the door, not certain who will open the door. It's disconcerting, Jacques."

"If you come when I tell you, there'll be no problem. Madeline doesn't pop in at odd hours. You're more likely to do that, Maîtresse. Hence it is better that you are never certain when she is here." He gave her a wide grin.

She tugged his beard hard enough for him to yelp.

"Enough, madame."

"Maîtresse," she reminded him.

"No, playtime is over." Jacques got out of bed.

"I'd like to change the next appointment," Marie said.

"Is this in retribution for my not telling when Madeline comes here?"

"*Mais non.* You think me that petty and puerile?"

Jacques gave a slight nod of his head, which she ignored.

"Thursday. Usual time, but Thursday."

"I must check. May I call you later?"

"I'll not be home. A suitor is taking me to dinner. Hint, hint."

"Madame, I am sculpting a statue of you. You want me also to feed you?"

"It would add some romance to our bumping and grinding."

"You bring the wine, madame, and I shall prepare lunch the next time we meet."

"Thursday?"

"While you're dressing, I'll check."

Jacques left the room, and Marie scrambled to her feet to quietly follow.

"Thursday," she heard him mutter. "I'll probably have to cancel someone for this bitch."

Marie prickled a bit but softly followed him to the studio, where he pulled a large ledger-type book from under a paint-stained canvas. After checking inside the book, he returned it to where it had been, and Marie managed to be half-dressed by the time he returned to the bedroom.

"Thursday is fine," he told her, crossing the floor to retrieve a fresh towel.

Once she heard the shower water come on, she ran

273

to the studio and found the appointment book. Madeline's name appeared under Tuesday at noon. She slipped the book back, and while passing the bathroom she bid Jacques a good-bye.

Sixty-two

"Louis," Marie shouted as she entered their home. "Louis."

"I'm in the dinning room, Marie."

She hurried to the dinning room and saw Sade seated at the big table. A bottle of expensive wine and a portion of a rack of lamb sat in front of him.

"Trying out your recipes again, Louis?"

"A new recipe actually. There's more in the kitchen, and there's enough wine for the two of us." He continued savoring the tender bloodred meat.

"You're generous tonight, Louis. Usually, you share your meals with the sluts you meet on the street."

"One slut is as good as another, Marie." Sade poured himself more wine. He missed the killer look that she bestowed on him.

"Louis, I saw Madeline today."

He stopped eating, and she had his full attention.

"Isn't this something you should tell Justin and not me?" he asked.

"She doesn't want to see Justin. She's frightened—even of Justin, I believe. Evidently, the man she left Justin for isn't treating her well, and she wants some help getting away from him."

Sade went back to his meal.

"Marie, I've lived this scenario before, only that time Justin played the hero."

"I'm not lying, Louis. She desperately wants to see you. Tomorrow at noon, she'll be modeling for Jacques."

"Jacques." Sade looked up at Marie. "Jacques has known her whereabouts all along. May I include you in the conspiracy?"

"I modeled today at Jacques's studio, and when I left I ran into her on the stairs."

"Jacques is having a busy day, *non?*"

"She only models. She doesn't fuck."

"That's what Jacques tells you." Sade offered Marie a sip of his wine. She refused.

"The day you saw the statue of Madeline, I knew you still had an interest in her. The gleam in your eyes outshined the lighting in the room. Don't you have a tiny bit of curiosity about what she wants and don't you think it possible that she might be willing to return to your bed? She's not had a man like you since she ran away from her little town." She saw Sade lean back in the chair and weigh what she had just said.

"To me Madeline is an enigma. She is beautiful, but

so hard to reach. She is delicate, but proved herself tough in her defense of Justin. Justin. Why wouldn't she go back to him?"

"He admitted not being able to fuck her. For the young the romance of purely sleeping side by side can wear thin. Did she lack an appetite for pleasuring her flesh?"

"Never," Sade said. He dropped his utensils onto the large dinner plate. "Tuesday at noon. She can't expect me to knock on Jacques's door."

"Jacques can work three hours at a stretch. He is paying her, and I doubt she stays longer than necessary. Three o'clock should be about right."

Marie left Sade picking at his food. She left the house by the back door to hurry directly to Justin's garret. She hoped the child would not be present. *Bothersome little bastard*, she thought. Relieved to find Justin alone, she set her trap.

"I'm frightened, Justin. Frightened and disappointed. Louis is the serial killer."

"Marie, I don't . . ."

"Wait, Justin. He's been raving about the house, destroying some of our best antiques. Cursing even at Lilliana. I believe he is mad. I think he is changing into one of those poor souls you kill on dark nights in the cemetery. You know, the vampires who go insane, losing all of their humanness. He no longer makes sense when he talks. Even Comte de Mirabeau—I mean Gerard—suspects Louis."

"Gerard believes the killer is mortal."

"Gerard came to the house the other day and re-minded me of how Louis often did things to be the center of attention. Drove me crazy when my daughter was alive. That's why I had Louis imprisoned and committed. Louis has always been on the edge of insanity."

"You and Sade have always fought, Marie."

"He let it slip that he was meeting Madeline tomorrow." She turned away from Justin and waited for her words to sink in.

"Has she been living with him, Marie?"

"She's not been at the house. He owns several houses in Paris, Justin. She must be living in one. Sometimes he doesn't come home for several days at a time."

"Where does he go?"

Marie shrugged. "He has a bad temper. I don't press some issues."

"You and Sade are constantly bantering. I can't believe you are afraid of him."

She walked closer to Justin.

"I am in your mother's body because Louis destroyed mine. He is stronger now than when he destroyed my body."

Justin reached out to touch her hair, but stopped and rested his hand on her shoulder instead.

"Do you know when he will be seeing Madeline tomorrow?"

"He is paying Jacques to sculpt a new statue of Madeline. She evidently agreed to pose."

"Sade told you this?"

"Louis has been raving on and off for several days. I finally pieced all of what he has said together."

"I'll take you home, Marie."

"To confront Louis?"

Justin continued to stare at her.

"*Non,* that will not do. You may never find Madeline," Marie said.

"But you say she is posing for Jacques. . . ."

"What are you going to do? Start a ruckus? Have neighbors call the gendarme? What if Madeline did have something to do with the deaths that have taken place in Paris? The gendarmes will show no mercy. What if Louis has already turned her? She won't rush into your arms."

"She didn't allow him to turn her before."

"Before doesn't mean forever, Justin. Catch them together tomorrow. They'll meet at three in front of Jacques's home. I can help you destroy Louis, but first, don't you want to find Madeline?"

SIXTY-THREE

"I'm sorry to bother you tonight, Monsieur Chartres, but I've been restless tonight and thought you might help put my mind at ease."

"*Oui.* Come in, Justin. I'm in the midst of a bit of housecleaning, but there may be an empty chair still for you." Jean searched the room with his eyes, spying a lone hassock shoved into a corner of the room. He retrieved the hassock and placed it in the center of the room. "This is the best I can do. I've been cleaning out closets and separating out the things I mean to give to charity."

"It's all right, I can stand. I didn't mean to intrude at this delicate time."

"You mean my wife's and son's clothes. It is something that must be done before my daughter comes home."

"Have the gendarmes found her?" Justin squatted down on the floor. Jean sat on the hassock.

"Thank God! They found Reginald, my brother-in-law, in England. He has Yvette. Babbette tricked my daughter into thinking I had needed to get away from all the memories. Yvette thought I had run to England, since I had gone to school there and still have friends there."

"All this time she has been safe, then."

"*Oui.* Babbette stayed behind to take care of some business. When she hadn't called Reginald or arrived on the date she was supposed to, he called the gendarme. He is flying back with Yvette tomorrow afternoon. I want the place to be a new home for Yvette. We need to continue with our lives. If this killer will let us."

"That is why I came. Have you remembered anything from the night you were attacked?"

"Bad breath is all I can recall. That and the horror on that poor gendarme's face."

"Did the killer have an accomplice?"

"Justin, I've been over this story many times with the gendarme. I grow tired of telling it and would rather banish it from my brain."

"Your daughter is returning to Paris, Jean. You can't afford to forget."

"I remember only the beast that knocked me to the ground, which I assumed was the same slight figure that carried off the gendarme."

"I found much blood on the cobblestones. It must have already started to drink before he carried off the gendarme."

"The gendarme's neck had been shredded. Of

course there had to be blood. They found the drained body five blocks from where I was attacked. The gendarmes were able to follow a trail of blood, Justin. It happened quickly. I had a lot of pain." Jean lifted the arm with the cast on it.

"There was no evidence of a woman?"

"This is no ordinary woman, if the beast even is female." Jean studied his visitor. "What makes you think a woman is involved?"

"Thank you, Monsieur Chartres." Justin stood. "May you and your daughter stay safe."

Jean watched the young man with stooped shoulders walk to the door.

"Justin? Do you suspect someone?"

The younger man leaned his head against the door frame. His shoulders shook. His hands folded into tight fists. Before Jean could reach him, Justin flung the door open and escaped.

Sixty-four

"I was afraid you wouldn't come home," Felix said as Justin closed the door to the garret. "Someday you won't, I know that."

"I wouldn't abandon you, Felix."

"No, but I worry that the day of your death is not far away. I dream about it sometimes."

"That's not comforting for either of us."

"Many bad people hate you. Many people with supernatural strength may want to end your life."

Justin sat in the chair.

"Ending my life would be too easy. True enemies would want me to stay alive."

"Turn you completely into a vampire?"

"I guess Gerard would think it true justice if I suffered the eternal hunger for blood. That's why I should be looking for another home for you. Maybe I've waited too long."

"No one else wants me." The boy shrugged. "Except for the perverts who visit that brothel you found me at."

"I don't even send you to school," Justin said.

"Don't worry, I've learned a lot since my parents died. I learned about things that I didn't believe existed. Want some fruit?"

"You've also learned thievery, because I know you had no money to buy anything."

"This is the old fruit that's about to go rotten. I asked the vendor if he'd let me have some for charity."

Justin stared at the boy.

"Okay, he gave me a few pieces, and I slipped some extra into the bag as I was leaving."

"Sit by me, Felix."

The boy came close and sat on the floor.

"You're especially sad tonight," Felix said. "More than you've been on other nights."

"In other words, I'm a sad sack to be around."

"You and I wonder where we fit in. I have no one, and you miss someone. We both know what we're missing, though."

"There you are wrong, Felix." Justin shifted out of the chair and sat on the floor. "We refuse to acknowledge what we do have. At least for a small period of time we have each other. What makes me sad is that it can't be forever."

"Why not?" the boy asked, furrowing his brow.

"Because I am not meant to be a father to anyone. You should have a good education and a family."

"Justin, I am almost fifteen years old. Most families

wouldn't welcome me into their homes the way you have, especially if they heard about where I come from."

"The brothel."

The boy nodded his head.

"I have no right to be here in Paris, and I miss home. If I go home, my uncles will see me dead. Help me, Justin."

"I want to but can't. I live a dangerous life. You'd . . ."

"In Paris, no one cares about me. Back home, my uncles fear I can take possession of my parents' land. I walk the streets of Paris and no one stares at me. I don't worry about bad accidents happening to me. Would you send me home to my death?"

Justin reached out and pulled the boy to his chest.

"*Non*, Felix, I would never send you to your death. For once I want to save a life instead of destroying it. All my life I thought death to be the only freedom. But you, Felix, deserve to thrive and start your own family."

Sixty-five

Sade recognized Jacques's house as soon as he saw it. The women chatting at the front door were the same as the last time he had been here. The loud noises of the street irritated his hearing. The scrawny children constantly got in his way.

He hadn't been sure that he could trust Marie, but after long thought he assumed he had nothing to lose by showing up. Could Madeline really need his help? A slight smile softened his face when he thought about how upset Justin would be to find Madeline back with Sade.

The women began screaming at their children, and Sade moved closer to the front door of the building to be out of the way of the scattering children.

"Monsieur Sade!"

He turned to see Madeline, her eyes clear, wide, but with a hint of sleepiness. She had lost weight, and her clothes were obviously secondhand.

"Madeline." He reached out for her hand, and she withdrew it from him.

"Why have you come here?" she asked.

Ah, Marie, what are you up to? he wondered.

"I came to offer my assistance. Marie mentioned you were selling your body to Jacques—"

"*Non!* I only pose for Jacques."

He knew it would do no good to argue with her.

"Posing for Jacques. I simply thought you might need additional monetary help."

"I'm not a prostitute, Monsieur Sade. I made the mistake of being your bed partner once, but I'll never do it again."

Sade noted that she hadn't let the front door close and could bolt whenever she wanted.

"*Mais non,* Madeline. I regret the scenes you had to be part of and the cheap women whom you met at my home. My life is very different now. I live with my mother-in-law and daughter."

"Your wife?"

"Been dead many years. I suppose that may have led me to the hedonistic life you saw. Losing one so dear."

"Monsieur Sade, I know now that you are a vampire, remember? Your phony excuses I won't abide."

"Am I losing my touch, Madeline? Or have I become too well known? That frown, Madeline—what is going through your head?"

"Walk with me. I will tell you why I pose for Jacques. And tell you about the further pain you have caused me. More painful than any of the whippings or bites."

To Sade's surprise, Madeline linked her arm with his.

Justin leaned against a stone building, watching Madeline and Sade draw closer together. They moved as one, stepping around the children, huddling closer for a passerby, and at times their faces almost touched. The crispness of Sade's clothes made Madeline's dress look like a rag. She didn't wear shoes, but she wore the tiny bracelet Justin had given her around her ankle. He wanted to rip the thing off her.

He managed to follow them for several blocks. However, the ache behind his eyes and the glare of the sun blinded him an instant too long. They had disappeared. He doubled back to Jacques's.

"Justin, what are you doing here?" asked Jacques.

"Did you know that Monsieur Sade meets Madeline downstairs?"

"Monsieur Sade? *Non*, you are wrong. She wouldn't be posing for me if she didn't have to. As far as I can tell, your sweetheart has another man. One that can't fend for himself. He must send a woman out to bring back money."

"All this time you've never said anything to me." Justin shook with the rising tide of his anger.

"For a while even madame managed to keep the secret, but now I see she finally broke down."

"Marie said she ran into Madeline yesterday when she left here."

"She's known from the first day. You think I enjoy giving my work away for free. Come with me."

Justin followed Jacques back to the studio. Jacques removed a canvas from an amorphous shape.

"This is Marie, Justin. We've been at this for over a month and this is as far as we've gotten. I don't believe that she wants me to create a statue of her. She comes here for . . ."

"Sex," Justin said.

"And not the everyday kind of sex."

"Have you tasted her blood?"

"I'm not a freak, Justin. She is, though." Jacques pushed back his hair and showed the bruises on his neck. "She takes more each time she comes."

"She'll continue taking more, Jacques, until she offers her own."

"She has. I've refused. Madame is uninhibited but strange. Often, I question whether I should continue this farce with her. The blood transfer is going too far."

"She's a vampire."

Jacques laughed.

"You mean the one that has been running around Paris?"

"At this point, I'm so confused I don't know." Justin saw a second figure wrapped in a fine cloth and walked to it. Before Jacques could stop him, Justin pulled the cloth off the figure and stood looking into Madeline's face. "You are having no problem duplicating Madeline."

"She is strictly business. Not that I wouldn't prefer

more." Justin turned and grabbed Jacques's shirt. "*Non,* Justin, I would not force myself on her. She is a beautiful woman and many men would like to—" Justin threw Jacques down on the floor. "Don't be angry at me, Justin. If you wish to fault anyone, then it should be yourself for not being able to hold on to her. From what you tell me, the foolish girl is getting money from several sources. What could she be doing for Sade? Can you imagine, Justin?"

Justin grabbed hold of the Madeline statute and swayed it back and forth.

"What are you doing, Justin? We've worked hard on that piece." Jacques pulled himself up onto his feet, but too late.

Justin had knocked the statue to the floor and stabbed the piece multiple times with a knife he had found on a table. Jacques stood back from the wild thrashing of Justin's arms. With his breath heaving, Justin fell to his knees.

Jacques walked back to Marie's statue and fingered the grooves.

"Would you like to destroy this one, too? I'm not fond of this one. The other I planned on keeping for myself . . . unless another buyer willing to pay enough came along. Then I could retire."

"Don't let Madeline come back."

"She'll be back in a few days. I have no way to contact her."

"Don't answer your door," Justin said.

"This will only drive her into deeper collusion with

Monsieur Sade. Do you want her dependent on him for all her money? Monsieur Sade did not appear to be a generous person. He will demand much from Madeline."

"She can say '*non*.'"

"Can she? Life isn't that easy. She loves deeply. Nothing will prevent her from getting what her lover needs. What would you do to have Madeline back? Is there anything you would say '*non*' to?"

Jacques watched Justin attempt to get to his feet. He would have helped the young man, but he still smelled anger in Justin's sweat. Holding on to a wall, Justin regained his footing.

"She'll be back at two on . . ."

"No, Jacques, I don't want to know."

"You'll not try to change her mind?"

"She chose Sade. I have no doubt that she will also choose his lifestyle."

"She is desperate, Justin. When desperate there aren't choices to make, only paths that must be traveled. Don't let Sade have her."

"Fight for her yourself, Jacques. She abandoned me."

Sixty-six

Gerard sat dozing on the steps that led up to Justin's garret and wondered whether he would be there all night. Guilt made him remain, no matter how long he had to wait.

He pricked up when he heard light footsteps on the stairs. He counted each floor climbed. Satisfied that the footsteps were headed for the top floor, Gerard stood to greet Justin.

"Gerard, what are you doing here?" Justin asked.

"The little ragamuffin wouldn't let me into your garret. Had to while the hours in this stinky, noisy hall. You don't have sophisticated neighbors, do you?"

"This is all they can afford, Gerard."

"Just because one can't afford a better place to live doesn't mean one should live like a pig."

Justin walked past Gerard, pulling his key from his jacket pocket.

"I wanted to warn you, Justin."

"A threat, Gerard?" Justin paused in opening the door.

"No, a warning about Marie. She despises you. You and Sade."

"We both know."

"I think she will come up with a scheme to pit you and Sade against each other. I made the mistake of telling her that I thought Sade might be the serial killer. She delighted in the idea, and I came away thinking it had been a ludicrous thought. If the killer is a vampire, it is probably young and inexperienced. Never trained, never guided. The vampire could have been made by a vampire with tainted blood who went insane."

"Make up your mind, Gerard."

The door suddenly opened in front of Justin.

"Don't listen to him, Justin. Come inside." Felix pulled at Justin's jacket.

"You are a foolish boy. Do you believe that you and Justin can hide from this problem? You both are in the center of it. Justin is a half-breed. I'd bet that he's more vampire than mortal now. He's spent his life among the undead, boy. You are marked to do the same." Gerard took a step toward the boy and laughed when Felix withdrew into the garret.

"Enough, Gerard. There's no bravery in scaring a child, especially a child who has gone through the life he has been forced to live. Go back to your moldy coffin. Lay your head on the satin pillow and pray that I never find you."

Sixty-seven

The quiet and the darkness of Jacques's apartment surprised Marie. Usually, he would play music as background even when he worked. She had never seen all the shutters tightly closed before. It felt like a grave, she thought, remembering when she first awoke to her vampirism.

"Are you in mourning, Jacques?"

"I'm not going to work with you, madame."

"We have an agreement."

"You broke it." Jacques led her into the studio. The remains of Madeline's statue still lay on the floor. "Justin paid a visit yesterday. He didn't have as much appreciation for my work as you do."

"And the statue I've been posing for?"

"I've destroyed it."

"What did Justin say?" Marie scooped up a sliver of clay from the floor.

"He said that Madeline has been meeting with your

friend Monsieur Sade. You've been playing us all for fools, haven't you, madame?"

"You couldn't live without Madeline. I allowed you to work with her."

"You bribed me. Granted, I weakened and fell into the trap. But it is finished."

"*Non*, it's not, Jacques." Marie moved closer to Jacques. Her fingernails painted a bright pink, glistened even in the darkened room. "We'll make love." He pulled away from her.

The room felt small to Marie, closed in, shrinking with every minute she stood here. The faraway sound of dirt being shoveled into her grave echoed from her past.

"First I will open the shutters and windows." She moved across the room, opening and unshuttering each window she came to. "Isn't that better, Jacques? You've been sitting here allowing yourself to wallow in other people's despair. We have our own lives. Let them parse out their own problems, for we have none."

"What will Sade do with Madeline?"

"Nothing he hasn't done before. I told you they were lovers in the past, before Justin rescued the poor damsel. Now she is playing one against the other. She would have played with you too, except she saw a way to get money from you without having to fuck you. Poor girl is probably tired, given her boyfriend and Sade. She's a fool, though, because I know what a keeper you are." Marie managed to trap Jacques into a corner. She let her hand wander down the front of his jeans. "For me," she whispered.

"I can't trust you, madame," he said coldly.

"And I can trust you?" she asked. "Jacques, we satisfy our desires without worrying about who we hurt. We know the joy of variety. We consider ourselves loners but still need a bit of security on our darkest days. Perfect mates, Jacques. Perfect mates."

"Madel—" Marie placed her hand over Jacques's mouth.

"An ignorant child. You want her because you can't get her. I know what that feels like. Watching others steal away her time from you. Imagining the feel of her hands on your body. Her movements slowly increasing in speed. Her sweat shining on her flesh. I've wanted another that much, Jacques. But I'll not play the fool for him anymore, because I have you."

"You make it sound like we're each settling for leftovers," he said.

Marie stripped in front of him. "Do I look leftover? They're incompetent lovers who fear true talent."

Sixty-eight

Madeline lifted Matthew's sleeping head and cradled it in her arms. She kissed his brow, the coldness of his flesh setting fire to the pit of her stomach.

"Destroy him," Sade whispered. "Destroy him before he turns you into the same pathetic creature he is."

"He's my brother, Monsieur Sade. He suffers because of the plague you have brought to France."

"The plague, as you call it, Madeline, is far older than I."

"You can save him, Monsieur Sade. I will do anything you want if you save him."

"I've already bedded you, Madeline. You offer nothing new. Even if you could, he is beyond help. A thing like him I would discard. He doesn't even sense danger. We walk in, you touch him, and still he sleeps."

"He trusts me to protect him."

"*Non*, Madeline. He doesn't have the true vampire senses."

"You can teach him. Please, teach him not to kill. Teach him to take a little of my blood each day. An amount that will permit both of us to survive."

Sade grabbed hold of her arms and forced her to her feet.

"I could change you, Madeline. What I teach you, you can pass on to your brother." He swept her hair back off her neck. He lifted her up and carried her to a room where he had seen a bed. Placing her gently on the bed, he fluffed the pillows beneath her head.

She allowed his hands to search her body, to open buttons, unzip zippers, slide the shabby clothes from her body. Her eyes looked as innocent as they had the first time he had taken her.

"The vampire world is easy to settle into, Madeline, if you have a guide. The world will be totally different after you pass over into death."

"I'll always be cold like you," she said.

"Not cold, frozen. Frozen into this world for eternity. Time will forget you exist. Days will be overwhelmingly bright, but nights will soothe the pain of the glare. Your tongue will sharpen to the taste of food. Still you'll have the hunger."

"My brother hates the hunger."

"Your brother didn't pass over easily, did he? Violence toyed with his mind. Fear gripped his soul into silence."

"Does he still have a soul, Monsieur Sade? Do you?"

"*Oui,* and it belongs solely to me. No God will rape me of that."

298

"Because no God would want your dark soul," she said.

"What will happen to your brother's soul? Can you martyr yourself and give him a constant companion?

"You are beautiful, Madeline. As a vampire, you will always look the way you do now. Never grow old, never gain a scar, nor lose any of your senses."

"I'll lose my humanity."

"Not even that will be lost to you, Madeline. My daughter refuses human blood and survives on animals. How human is that?"

"You made your own daughter a vampire?"

Sade began to undress.

"I wanted her with me, just as you want to keep your brother with you. Maybe there is no afterlife for mortals. Maybe they fall into a black abyss and completely disintegrate into dust. Only we vampires survive. Are you sure there is a God waiting for you? There is a brother begging for your help." Naked, Sade dropped onto the bed. He rolled on top of her to remind her of the size and weight of him. "I recollect the soft, wet feel between your legs. The way you thrust forward to meet me." He touched the pulse on her neck. "Do you retain the memory of how I tasted?" He rolled onto his back and pressed her head down toward his penis. She didn't fight him.

The old bed leaned to one side, offering a precipice of danger for mindless lovers. The dark of the room hid the shambles that surrounded Sade and Madeline.

Sade heard the rustle of rats, the creaking of wood

being destroyed by termites, the scurry of vermin free to multiply and infest, but best of all, he heard the soft beating of Madeline's heart. The blood rushed through her veins, teasing him with its fresh scent and health. Unadulterated blood slipping through channels feeding her organs.

Reaching down, Sade grabbed her mass of red hair and pulled Madeline up to taste her lips. One lip he bit, and the sweetest blood spilled into his mouth. He would make this last through the night, and take her life only when he'd sated himself on her pain and fear.

"Do it now," she pleaded.

"*Non,* Madeline. By the end of the night, you will cut your own veins open and beg me to take what little blood flows through your veins." He rolled her onto the floor and settled heavily on top of her. "You must pay for the gift I offer."

"Isn't giving you my life enough?" she asked.

"The life you give up is inferior to the one I bring to you. Feel the wood against your back, Madeline. That is how hard your body feels against my flesh, but by morning you will give way to my every whim. There will be no barrier to my demands."

Sade pulled a sheet from the bed and started to shred the material into strips. He saw the fear in her eyes turn to resignation and savored the willingness of his victim.

Sixty-nine

Jacques couldn't understand Marie's frustration. Every orgasm she had strengthened her desire for more. He satisfied her with sex toys, whippings, and his mouth when his penis wilted, attempting to hide from her greedy grasp.

"My blood," he whispered in her ear, remembering how that often sated the nymphomaniac in her. But she always refused.

"I've tasted you many times, Jacques. Now you must drink from me." She bit hard on her forearm and offered Jacques the blood that spilled rivulets onto her white flesh.

"I cannot," he said, drawing himself up into a seated position. "The idea disgusts me. I don't know why you are so insistent, Maîtresse. There are limits for all of us, although we still haven't established what yours are."

"I want you to come to me willingly, Jacques. I want you to taste my blood."

"How many men have agreed to your unusual request?"

"The other men don't matter. I needed them only to keep myself from paling and weakening. You must be more than that. You must take the place of the man who obsesses me."

"I'm not a substitute." Jacques swung his legs over the side of the bed. He felt her hands encircle his neck. "We've moved on to asphyxiation. Will your appetite ever be appeased?" He attempted to move, but her strong grip prevented him. He raised his hands to cover hers, thinking he could easily undo her grasp, but could not.

She leaned against his body and whispered, "Once you've tasted my blood, you will never stop drinking."

"I don't want to start any new bad habits," he said. "As you know, I have quite a few already."

"My blood will give you a life you've never dreamed existed. A never-ending life that will take you through the many ages of mankind."

"Your blood, madame, can only stick in my throat and cause my stomach to roil. Even the smell of blood causes my belly to turn queasy. Watching it drip down your arm doesn't help to render me romantic."

"I could kill you, Jacques. I could take all your blood and leave your body dry and eternally dead."

Jacques broke out in a sweat. Her threat mirrored the murders taking place in Paris. What did he know about this woman of unequaled strength? Her lips touched the pulse of his neck and the sweat became a cold chill.

"Give me time, madame. The concept of drinking blood is something I have never contemplated."

"You have little time, Jacques. The years pass quickly. I can almost smell the stink of your body in its grave."

Jacques remained still, afraid any movement would send her into a fury. Her tongue licked at the flesh on his neck like a kitten, her tongue rough and dry.

"Have others refused you, madame?" *And what have you done about it?* he asked silently.

"Why would anyone refuse what I can give?" she asked.

"Everyone eagerly laps at your blood?"

"I don't offer my precious blood to everyone. You are the chosen, Jacques." She let go of his neck and let her arms travel down his shoulders, bringing the sight of her open wound into view. "See how red and thick it flows."

"The wound is closing up," he said, awed by the sight.

"But it can be opened up again. I will bleed for you, Jacques, if you promise not to waste a drop of my blood."

"I need my energy for the morning. I have several students due tomorrow."

"You'll feel the super power my blood can give. Take but a few drops tonight, and next time we see each other I assure you that you will crave more."

Her body iced his flesh, and he remembered Justin's last visit. He had laughed when Justin indicated that Marie could be a vampire. Justin had not laughed.

"Why is your body so cold, madame?"

"Maîtresse," she reminded him as she nudged her face into his neck.

"Of course. Maîtresse."

"Doesn't it excite you?" She giggled, drunk with sex.

"Are you human, Maîtresse?"

"Here I am baring my flesh, my blood, my heart to you, Jacques, and you ask if I am human. I'm certainly not a dreary robot mechanically pleasuring you."

"I've never heard the beat of your heart," he said.

She freed him and lay back on the sheet.

"Come, Jacques, lay your head upon my breast and imagine the sound. You've never listened closely enough to recognize the secret beat that keeps me tied to the earth."

He turned to look at her. She had beauty. Yet he had never been able to appreciate it. Why? he wondered. What did she lack? Her white, unblemished skin glowed in the darkness of the room. Her features couldn't be more perfect. She invited with a smile that couldn't be duplicated by most other women. But her voice held a warning.

"Rest, Jacques. We both are worn out. Take comfort on my breast." She opened her arms wide.

He stood.

"Not tonight. I must walk for a while." He began to dress.

304

"It's dangerous on the streets. Come back to bed."

Tonight he feared his own bed more than the empty streets of Paris.

Jacques left Marie sprawled across his bed. He hoped she would be gone by the time he returned. He wouldn't return home until minutes before his student's appointment.

He remembered the address where Madeline and Justin had lived together and headed in that direction. He constantly checked the street around him, looking for a hint of anything that moved, but caught sight of only a very pregnant calico cat.

Justin's building did not try to lock out intruders. He easily walked into the hallway and climbed the stairs to the garret. He knocked several times before a sleepy Justin came to the door.

"Jacques, what are you doing here?"

Jacques checked over his shoulder, expecting to see Marie's furious ghost about to attack.

"Please, may I come in?" Jacques asked.

"Try not to make much noise. My child is asleep."

Jacques nodded and walked past Justin. Odd, he thought, he didn't know that Madeline and Justin had a child. He guessed the screen hid the bed. Justin prevented him from walking anywhere near the screen.

"Tell me what you want, Jacques."

The young Justin looked very old. Ancient. Worn out. Ready to be laid to rest.

"You mentioned that Marie is a vampire. Is she?"

"What has she done?" Justin asked.

"She insists I taste her blood."

"And you have?"

"*Non,* I refused."

"She let you?"

"She wants me to come to her of my own desire. Justin, her flesh is frigid. I don't ever remember hearing the beat of her heart, although she offered to have me lie on her breast and listen."

"You would have heard nothing but her lies telling you that you needed to listen harder. One taste of her blood and you would treasure the silence."

"How could that be?"

"You would be hers."

Jacques shook his head. "All this is wrong. I even suspected her of being the serial killer that is rampaging through the city. She could have killed me. Her power is almost superhuman."

"Not almost, Jacques. Is. You must either stake her or run. But she will look for you, and if she does find you, your life will end."

"Are you telling me to kill Marie?"

"She is already dead, Jacques. You'll only be destroying something that should have never existed."

"I can't. What if you're wrong? The gendarmes would be at my house. They'd take me away to prison."

"The vampires survive on mortal doubts."

"She should be gone from my place by morning, and by afternoon, so will I."

SEVENTY

Jacques swore that he would walk the streets until morning. Justin offered to give the artist space on the floor, but Jacques couldn't remain still. He needed to act now, but couldn't. He needed too many things from his apartment. The artist nervously paced the width of the room until his hand finally caught hold of the door-knob. He thanked Justin, hoped Justin would find Madeline, and left.

Justin couldn't go back to sleep but had no energy. He dropped into a chair and stared at the walls. Could Madeline be with Sade tonight? If she were, would she swallow Sade's blood? Had she already? No, he could still sense her free will out there, and her pain. Physical pain. Mental pain. They blended into one.

"Find her, Justin."

He turned to see Felix out of bed.

"You'll never rest if you don't find her." Felix moved closer and touched Justin's face. "The lines

307

grow deeper. Your eyelids heavier. And the skin on your face hangs slack."

"My body can't move past the front door, Felix. Every muscle aches. My flesh throbs in pain. All I can do is sit here."

The frown on Felix's face turned into fear.

"Maybe it's not your own pain you feel. Perhaps Madeline calls to you."

"She isn't calling for my help. There is resignation and desire for a swift end."

"Give her your strength. Find her. Make her want to live again."

A breath caught in Justin's throat, finally returning when a sharp pain had passed. He fought the malaise and stood. Felix pushed a jacket into his hands.

"What if she doesn't want me anymore? She may be tired of the mortal life."

"I don't know her, Justin. Is she capable of wanting the vampire life?"

Even if she were, Justin decided he could not desert her.

SEVENTY-ONE

Tied to the foot of the bed, her legs spread apart by the strips of sheet that bound her ankles to the heating pipes, Madeline looked up at the ceiling. Brown stains spotted the ceiling where rain had dripped through the old roof. Paint peeled into misshapen thin slices dangling precariously from the crumbling plaster.

She had managed to muffle most of her cries. Her body suffered, but far less than her heart ached. Once again, she meekly played toy to Sade's childish and cruel fantasies. She feared he would kill her without changing her. Where would that leave her brother?

Sade stroked her cheek with the back of his hand.

"You'll not die, Madeline, at least not forever. You'll wake hungry and frightened. A new babe seeking her parent's protection. I'll be beside you. Shall I take you back to my home, or do you prefer this . . ." Sade looked around the room. ". . . hovel?"

"I want to stay near my brother." Her voice sounded so soft that she wondered whether Sade could hear her.

"Your brother. I think once you know what a true vampire is, you will abandon him."

"Never." The word caught in her throat, catching a sob from deep within her body. "Please end this now," she pleaded.

She saw Sade go still.

"What is it? Monsieur Sade, what's wrong?"

Her image vanished from his eyes, and instead she saw flames.

"My blood. Take more of my blood." Even she heard the panic in her voice.

"A true vampire, Madeline, hears, sees, and senses a world a mortal can never know."

Madeline pulled on the material that bound her near numb arms to the bed. Pain shot up her thighs when she tried freeing her legs.

"Leave him be," she demanded.

"I've not moved." His voice was innocent, his eyes now on fire.

She heard the confused footsteps pacing the hall, tripping over familiar objects.

"He knows you are here, Monsieur Sade."

"And?"

"Don't hurt him. I've allowed you the use of my body. Keep your part of the bargain." She wanted to call out, scream the words "go away," but instead she lay silent, not wanting to attract the person she knew would come.

"What was the bargain, Madeline? I only remember promising a night of luxurious agony before gifting you in the morning." He cocked his head and kept staring at her.

Looking past Sade's shoulder, Madeline saw her brother in the doorway. The hunger darkened his expression, and the smell of her blood caused saliva to drip from his gaping mouth.

"Go away, Matthew. Monsieur Sade is helping us. He'll make me a vampire, teach me how to survive, and I will teach you. Go away until it is over."

Matthew took several steps into the room.

"Matthew, there is nothing you can do here. Go back to your room and wait." The words scratched her throat.

"He's drawn your blood, Madeline. He's opened wounds on your body." Matthew sounded dazed.

"I agreed to this. He didn't force me," she said. She looked back at Sade. He stared into her eyes. The fire in his eyes smoldered, then burst into new flames. "Destroy me, Monsieur Sade, not my brother."

"And what will he do without you?"

"He's done this before to you, hasn't he?" Matthew asked.

"Not quite. I think we've surpassed our other rendezvous. Listen to your sister, Matthew, go away and play with a weak mortal that can't harm you. You must be hungry. People coming home from a late-night show and workers needing to meet early schedules are beginning to fill up the streets. Ah, if you listen properly, Matthew, you'll hear the click of high heels on the cobblestone streets."

"Free my sister." Matthew's sinister tone made Madeline wince.

She knew her brother couldn't survive a direct conflict with Sade. Even with her soul blackened by the night spent with Sade, she prayed to God. She asked God to save a killer while she waited to become the same herself.

"He's a fool, Madeline. You shouldn't really miss him."

"You don't have to kill him," she said.

"I can't—he's already dead. But I can destroy what he has left." Sade lowered his head to kiss Madeline on the forehead.

She knew Sade meant to provoke her brother.

"Leave, Matthew, leave," she screamed, her voice cracking with the effort.

Matthew rushed Sade in a blur of movement. Her brother's hands wrapped around Sade's throat. Sade's face turned into a horrible mask of glee. His features lit up with the flash of the power rekindling his body.

Matthew let go of Sade long enough to touch his sister's swollen cheek.

"You're so beautiful, Madeline. How could you let him?" her brother asked before being thrown across the room by Sade's straightened back.

"You promised you'd help me save my brother," she said, wishing she could free her hands to grab Sade's rising body.

"Nonsense, Madeline," Sade said before Matthew's body slammed into him.

She watched her brother fight, but Sade merely flicked Matthew aside. Sade's laughter echoed over and over in the room until her ears rang from the sound. The laughter encouraged the boy to attack carelessly. Matthew tried to land a punch, but Sade gripped the boy's fist and ripped the hand from the arm. Blood dripped from the opening. Without the beating of a heart, the blood slowly fell to the floor, and the burgundy color splashed onto Sade's naked flesh. The hand fell onto Madeline's abdomen, chilling her body with the icy coldness of Matthew's flesh.

"Matthew, run," she screamed.

The boy held his handless arm out to his sister, a look of surprise freezing for a second on his face.

"Help me," he whispered so softly that she had to read his lips.

"Pick up your hand, boy." Sade circled around behind Matthew. "Maybe vampires can reattach limbs. You could try. Go, pick it up." Sade toppled Matthew down upon Madeline.

The weight of her brother's body drove the breath from her lungs. His blood mingled with her own, his hand rolling against her right breast.

"Matthew, take the hand and run. You can staunch the blood with some rags." She lowered her voice to a whisper. "He means to destroy you."

"Little by little." Sade stamped a foot down on

Matthew's back and pried the boy's right leg from his body.

"Madeline, Madeline," Matthew cried, and buried his head between her breasts.

She looked at Sade covered in her brother's blood.

"Finish him," she pleaded.

Sade grabbed the boy's hair and yanked hard enough to break the neck, but didn't stop until he held Matthew's head high in the air as the boy's body fell to the floor.

"I won't go through with this bargain," she said. "You've deceived me."

"You did right in bringing me here, Madeline. I did what you could not. In your heart you always knew that he couldn't be saved. Will you thank me, Madeline?" Sade set Matthew's head on the floor next to her own. "I'm sure you'll want a few minutes of privacy to say good-bye to your brother. Maybe you could even say a prayer, although it will be useless." Sade left the room.

Madeline turned her face toward her brother's head. His long lashes curled up over his eyelids made her want to reach over and shut his eyes, but she couldn't. His bloodied nose looked misshapen, and his parted lips appeared ready to speak. She thought she saw a nerve in his cheek tweak. She strained her eyes to catch another slight movement. Nothing.

When Sade returned, his flesh sparkled from the use of soap and water. He dressed without saying a word, without a passing glance at Madeline. Once dressed, he walked to the doorway and stopped. He didn't turn to face her.

"Think about what happened tonight, Madeline. As the shadows in this room ebb and flow, think about every action, every word." He crossed the threshold and disappeared.

Realizing that Sade meant to leave her tied, Madeline found her own voice. "Sade! Sade!" she screamed.

SEVENTY-TWO

Justin stumbled most of the night through the dark streets. His head pounded, and his flesh crawled with the feel of sharp needles. He ached. From time to time, he reached out to touch a wall to stabilize himself.

He turned one corner and thought he heard footsteps, but when he looked around no one could be seen. Only old, dilapidated buildings loomed over him, their ornamentation sliding from their skins.

Where's the dawn? he wondered. He anticipated daylight, hoping it would drive away the ghosts inside his head.

"Ah, how lucky for Madeline that I ran into you."

Justin recognized Sade's voice, but at first couldn't see him until Sade suddenly appeared in front of him.

"Where's Madeline?" Justin asked. "Is she still mortal?"

"What is so precious about mortality? Yes, she can

die as any mortal can, and she might if you don't go to her."

"Where?" Justin's body flushed hot and his hands sweated.

"End of the block, go right two blocks. Ugly house with a dreadful color painted on its shutters. Who knows, maybe the color wasn't so bad when the paint was fresh. I left the door open, and over the doorway there's a hawk. Big beak, large talons. It probably had held something, but it broke off long ago."

Justin walked past Sade, hearing the vampire drone on about architecture and the poor taste of the bourgeoisie. Justin turned right and walked the two blocks Sade had indicated. At the end of the street, he recognized the blood stain left by the gendarme. He had been this close to her once before, when he had met the old man. Had she watched him? Had she wanted him to go away?

A door stood open to the house on his right. He walked closer and saw the hawk over the doorway. He kept walking until he stood in the hallway of the house. The overpowering fetid smell made him hesitate.

"Madeline," he yelled over and over, not bothering to stop and listen until finally he made out the sound of a frail voice. He climbed the stairs, preparing himself for the horror Sade had left behind. The smell worsened as he drew closer to the frail voice calling his name.

In the room at the end of the hall, he found Madeline tied both to the foot of a bed and heating pipes, her

317

skin a mass of wounds and welts, blood hardening into faded stains. Next to her face lay a head.

Justin rushed forward and undid the bonds and helped her to lower her arms, the pain of the movement showing in her face. Next his hands worked quickly at the bonds wrapped around her ankles.

She managed to roll onto her side, her face now inches from whoever the boy had been.

"Matthew."

Madeline whispered the name, and Justin immediately remembered all the times that she had spoken of her brother.

"You left me for him," Justin said.

She looked over her shoulder. "I had to. I wanted him to stop killing."

"Vampire" was the only word he spoke.

"I thought Sade could help. I wanted him to teach my brother how to survive without killing. Matthew refused to take my blood."

"Did Sade change your brother?"

"*Non*. He destroyed him." Her shaking hands reached out to touch her brother's cheeks.

"I'll burn the body, Madeline."

"*Non,* we must bury him."

Justin shook his head. "If you want to be sure that he's found peace, you must let me burn him."

"I'll do it with you," she said, removing her hands from her brother. She turned to Justin and reached out to touch his arm.

Justin winced.

"I'm sorry. I needed to take care of my brother."

"You watched Matthew kill and never came to me. Instead, you turned to Sade." His rigid body became tenser.

"I knew you would destroy Matthew. I thought Sade would save him."

"That is why you once again gave yourself to Sade?"

She looked down at the floor between them.

"*Oui,* Justin. He offered to make me a vampire and teach me how to survive so that I could pass the lessons on to my brother."

Justin pulled away from her.

"I didn't know what else to do, Justin." She looked up at him. "Your face is made of stone."

Justin stood.

"I think it's better if I take care of your brother alone. You won't want to watch the fire."

"Help me, Justin, don't abandon me."

"I said that I would take care of Matthew. Wash up and find some clothes for yourself." Justin pulled the few covers from the bed to wrap the body parts.

"Am I ugly?" she asked.

"You're battered," he replied, pausing to look toward the boarded up window. "I'll help to get you some medical care." He continued with his task.

"And where shall I go after that?" she asked, rising to stand.

"You can stay at a charity house until you're well enough to work."

"Take me back." She reached out to him but didn't dare to take a step in his direction.

She couldn't bear to see him back away again, he knew.

"I have a child living with me. He is an orphan and can't return to his own country. I rescued him from a brothel."

"We'll look for a larger place."

Justin looked at her.

"How many times did you watch Matthew kill? Can you count the number? Or has it all become a blur to you? The faces of the victims lost in the selfishness of holding on to your brother.

"Do you expect me to sleep next to you? Eat at the same table? Take you home to a child when blood covers you?"

"I expect you to love me," she said.

"You see what love did, Madeline?" He pointed to the various parts of her brother's body.

"Should I have been a coward like you, Justin?" She walked straight toward him, her eyes shaped into vengeful slits. "Should I have waited until he slept and then staked him through the heart and left him for another vampire to find? Your mother's body is being used by a murderer, a whore. When you look at Marie, does it warm your heart? I didn't want that for my brother. Are you that much better than me?"

Justin closed his eyes to see his mother as she once had been. Mother at peace, resting before another night of slaughter. He gripped his hands, feeling the stake's rough wood leaving tiny splinters in his skin. This time he couldn't lift his arms—the pain made him too weary. Still his mother's high-pitched scream rang in his ears. The stake easily pierced his mother's soft breast, finding her darkened heart. Briefly, her eyes opened to stare back at her betrayer. He felt her hands touch his cheeks. No—not his mother's hands, but Madeline's.

"I've always loved you, Justin. I forgave what you are, what you did to our small town, and I can even forgive the fact that you caused my brother's pain. *Oui,* that night that we fled, a vampire changed Matthew into a beast. We both ran that night and didn't try to help anyone we left behind."

Justin opened his eyes and grabbed Madeline close to him. Her bruised and cut flesh made his hands squeeze harder.

"I must be hurting you," Justin said, trying to pull away.

"You holding me heals me," she whispered, her arms tightening around his shoulders.

"I'm sorry, Madeline. I've buried myself in my own crusade in order to forget the pain. I buried the human part of me. In choosing to do that, I put a distance between us that should never have been there. Forgive me, Madeline."

Madeline's head rose from his chest as she looked at him. He wanted her and wanted to share a complete life with her, and *would.*

FIEND

JEMIAH JEFFERSON

In nineteenth-century Italy, young Orfeo Ricari teeters on the brink of adulthood. His new tutor instructs him in literature and poetry during the day and guides him in the world of sensual pleasure at night. But a journey to Paris will teach young Orfeo much more. For in Paris he will become a vampire.

Told in his own words, this is the story of the life, death, rebirth and education of a vampire. No one else can properly describe the endless hunger or the amazing power of the undead. No one else can recount the slow realization of what it means to grasp immortality, to live on innocent blood, to be a fiend.

THE TRAVELING VAMPIRE SHOW
RICHARD LAYMON

It's a hot August morning in 1963. All over the rural town of Grandville, tacked to the power poles and trees, taped to store windows, flyers have appeared announcing the one-night-only performance of The Traveling Vampire Show. The promised highlight of the show is the gorgeous Valeria, the only living vampire in captivity.

For three local teenagers, two boys and a girl, this is a show they can't miss. Even though the flyers say no one under eighteen will be admitted, they're determined to find a way. What follows is a story of friendship and courage, temptation and terror, when three friends go where they shouldn't go, and find much more than they ever expected.

__4850-7 $6.99 US/$8.99 CAN

THE DEMONOLOGIST

MICHAEL LAIMO

Is Bev Mathers going crazy? He's been hearing chilling voices in his head, seeing nightmarish visions that just can't be true. And it keeps getting worse and worse. No, unfortunately for Bev, he's completely sane. What's taking control of him is far more terrifying than insanity. And it has an unimaginable purpose....

Bev has become an innocent pawn in an infernal game, a victim of hellish forces beyond understanding. His visions of blood and debauchery are growing more ghastly every day. Some of them—the most shocking—are real. Bev can feel his mind, his body, his very soul slipping away. Will his only hope or his eternal damnation come from...the demonologist?

DOUGLAS CLEGG
THE ABANDONED

There is a dark and isolated mansion, boarded-up and avoided, on a hill just beyond the town of Watch Point in New York's Hudson Valley. It has been abandoned too long and fallen into disrepair. It is called Harrow and it does not like to be ignored. But a new caretaker has come to Harrow. He is fixing up the rooms and preparing the house for visitors....

What's been trapped inside the house has begun leaking like a poison into the village itself. A teenage girl sleeps too much, but when she awakens her nightmares will break loose. A little boy faces the ultimate fear when the house calls to him. A young woman must face the terror in her past to keep Harrow from destroying everything she loves. And somewhere within the house a demented child waits with teeth like knives.

JAMES A. MOORE
RABID GROWTH

People change all the time. But Chris Corin is noticing some pretty extreme changes in the people around him. His best friend is suffering from a strange fever and acting in ways that just don't make sense. And some oddly familiar people in town have started stalking Chris, blaming him for bizarre changes they've noticed in themselves.

Things get worse when the changes become physical. Hideous mutations appear around town. Can these changes somehow be responsible for the violent murders that have occurred—murders that point directly at Chris? Something definitely wants Chris dead, something very powerful.
